Nick Delmedico

SWORD OF FIRE

A division of d+2

Manufactured in the United States of America
Cover illustration by Kim Varela

Sword of Fire
Fiction, Fantasy

ISBN 978-1-58884-020-2

Dedicated to all the angels that have helped me on this journey through life, including:

Nancy Kudera

Gu'uh and Ginky

Carmine Spinarelli

John Layton Eklond and his mother Jane

Mary Malloy

Chris Wilder

Mr. and Mrs. Tunks

Sue Steinhauser

Jo Ann Dunaway

All the residents at the Crayon Palace Asylum

Mike Kessler, who always encouraged me

David Caylor and Angel Bunny, without whom this novel would never have been written.

Kathy Turner, Angel of Flight

Leah Spoelman

Dr. Katrina Iiams-Hauser

My son, fellow writer, and creative consultant, Nick

And mostly, my wife and partner, Becky.

Acknowledgement

This book, despite being a work of fiction, is littered with research. The views and religion presented here are not meant to offend. They are products of my own imagination and beliefs. This includes the idea that there are as many ways to God as there are people. Thus, all beliefs should be respected.

The story of the Fallen Angels can be found in the Apocrypha, the Lost Books of the Bible. In addition to popular mythology, I drew heavily upon Gustav Davidson's *A Dictionary of Angels* (1967, The Free Press). Legends of the Neutral Angels and the Holy Grail abound on the Internet. In short, there is an incredible amount of information and literature about angels.

I believe in angels. Some are alive and working with us in physical form. Others function behind the scenes in realms we know little about. Who knows what mysteries the Universe holds? We can only dream and imagine.

Nick Delmedico, November 2015

Sword of Fire

By Nick Delmedico

Prologue: Things to Come

Long before the time of Earth and Man, when the Universe was young, God created Angels, knowing that they were imperfect and that a third of them would betray Him and fall from grace. And therein lays a mystery, for God withheld grace from them, allowing the seeds of discontent to find fertile ground and hasten the fall. But who are we to question these workings, for even angels are denied knowledge of the inmost thoughts of the Divine.

Much later, God proclaimed, "Let there be Light." And there was Light. And what was there before this? Has darkness always been the canvas upon which God paints a masterpiece?

One more perplexing thought: Where does the darkness go in the presence of the light? Is it not still there, quietly waiting for the right moment to return?

1. My Affliction Revealed

"Do angels die?"

My daughter asks me difficult questions these days. She is thirteen going on twenty, with just enough innocence to favor the child in her. It's just that childish things and careful explanations no longer satisfy her, and lately she hungers for more knowledge of the world in which she lives.

"Do angels die?" she asks again. There is sincerity behind her eyes betraying a mind that thinks deep on these questions.

Then there is my side of this dilemma. I am caught between my image of her as a child, and my increasing awareness that she is anything but a child.

"What do you think?" I ask her.

There is a bottomless pause of silence between us. "You're stalling," she says. "You don't know."

She looks at me with deep focused eyes, something I have not seen before. They probe beneath my skin and I feel something churning within me, stirring the detritus of deep, forgotten memories. I taste bitter thoughts, things best left undisturbed. She senses it, too, trying to latch onto it and explore it with adult curiosity. I block her, turning my gaze outward, trying to focus on her instead.

She is a beautiful child, her face framed with ringlets of curls that shine with filaments of light. Her cheeks glow in natural color, her skin is as smooth as polished marble. She is over half my height, standing tall in her gait, her wings strong and full but still short and nubbed as they often are with younger angels. At the moment she is anything but a child. Her face is scrunched and her youthful features hide beneath furrowed brows. Her marble skin is cracking with deep lines of thought.

"Have you ever seen an angel die?" she asks.

She looks at me with probing eyes that seem to know the answer. Something has occurred between us and I can no longer hide my thoughts from her. My walls are glass, shattering under the weight of her inspection, and I am powerless to stop it. Her question has triggered something in me, primal feelings that angels should not hold. I feel a flash of fear and uncertainty.

Deep in the floodwaters of my past there are events that have visited my life and never left. Unwelcome guests. Like scars within me that refuse to heal, they ache now that she has touched them. How can something be that permanent? How have I kept these things hidden from her for so long?

She looks at me, waiting for an answer. Meanwhile I stare through a rift in my personality, a flaw through which pour the demons of my past. She leans closer. Staring into my eyes, as deep as any crystal gazer, as reflective as any pool of still water, she shares my vision.

I see angels fighting angels, brothers striking each other with horrible weapons. Something burns beside me, the smell overpowering. With fear I realize it is a flaming body, an angel on fire twisting in agony. I hear a muffled scream burst from it, barely audible over the sounds of the fighting around me.

She hears them too, echoes through time, the clash of combat, cries of pain, and the sound of Heaven cracking beneath her feet. I shield her, wondering how she has been transported beside me into this nightmare. I can hide her eyes but not her ears. She lives these moments with me, the sounds magnified in her imagination beyond anything real. I turn my head away from her hoping to break the trance. Instead I find myself looking into the bloodied face of my enemy. His cheeks and lips are contorted with rage as he screams at me. It startles me and breaks my concentration.

We are back in our garden, alive in the ever present now. I draw a deep breath and look at my daughter. My nightmare has ended and I am temporarily released. The serenity of the garden slowly fills my soul as the memories seep back into seclusion.

"What was that?" she asks. "Where were we just now?"

"Inside my mind," I say.

She stares at me in disbelief. "Oh, Father," she says, her lips heavy with sadness and pity. A single word escapes in a whisper. "How?"

"Not, how," I say. "But when. These are ancient images from a forgotten war."

"What war?"

"The one which divided us forever," I say.

"You were there?" she asks. "The battle at the beginning of time? The fight against the Fallen Angels?"

"I lived during that time, but I chose not to participate in the conflict."

"Then what are these visions?"

"Memories," I say. "Scant more than dreams."

Her eyes narrow and my insides squint like a blind man in the daylight. "How long have you had these dreams?" she asks.

"Ever since the battle," I say. "It is why we live on the outskirts of Heaven in this sparsely populated region. We are far from where the battle took place." I draw another deep breath vainly inhaling the peace and serenity of my garden. It is forced, empty and without satisfaction. "I sometimes infect my fellow angels just as I have you, another reason we live alone." I reach out and touch her shoulder. "Don't worry, you will not have an episode on your own. This disease is mine alone and cannot spread, but you may experience more visions in my presence, now that you are aware of them."

She hugs me with a daughter's love. "It won't keep me away from you, if that's what you're worried about." I feel her squeeze me tighter and all is right in Heaven. She releases me and continues her dialog, a thousand questions still ready to spring from her lips. "You didn't fight? Where were you then? If you were not at the battle, where do these visions come from? How do you know so much about the war if you didn't participate?"

I interrupt her. Where to start? "The visions are a gift from my brother," I say. "He gave me his memories, along with a thousand others. I see the battle from every viewpoint."

"Your brother?" she asks. "I have an uncle?"

Something else I have kept from her. I take another empty breath, trying to calm myself. Like spilled blood, I feel the memories pooling at the bottom of my mind. There will be another episode soon. It builds like clouds, the aura of an epileptic seizure. She feels it, too. Her eyes are fixed on infinity. She stares right through me, seeing what I refuse to look at. I tremble, naked before her gaze.

She sees something. I watch her eyes widen with amazement, then grow vapid with trepidation. "So," she says, her voice slow and trancelike. "Angels can bleed. And what bleeds can also die. Is this not true?"

"Perhaps," I say. "I suppose so. But there are things worse than death."

"What can be worse than death?" she asks.

I am a somnambulist, a victim of my own art. Her question draws another vision from my past and the Grand Mal is upon me. My mind answers her question, conjuring a fate worse than death.

I am transported back to that battlefield of long ago, fighting off attackers, fending for our lives. She is beside me as they advance towards us, a thunderous herd bent on our destruction. I fear I cannot protect her. The sound of their weapons clang and clatter, a bitter music that announces an end to the peace in Heaven. I know many of them, friends lost in the politics of Paradise, yet they come at me with unbridled hatred. Fortune shines, for I am not alone and the defenders of Heaven stand beside us. I know them by name, Johel, Quelamia, Kabshiel, Yaasriel, Semalion, the list goes on. Angels dedicated to this cause.

The enemy draws near and beneath the hatred on their faces I recognize many I count as friends:

Marchosias, Segef, Iabiel, and sweet Auza, a playful angel who once flirted with me. They cry in shrill voices meant to strike fear in our hearts. My comrades take firm footing and we meet the advancing army with a clash as deafening as any storm. As comrades fall before me I ask myself the same question she has asked.

2. Do Angels Die?

The battle rages about me. I know it is in my mind, but it is as real to me as anything. I know it is real for my daughter as well. She clings to my robes and I can no longer hide her from these horrors. All I want to do is flee this vain confrontation. I see no honor in fighting my friends, all of them angels who once worshiped God Almighty beside me. The conflict is everywhere, in every direction. Blades swoop beside us and I instinctively become a living shield to protect her. I push her safely behind the shifting lines of conflict. Eager faces brush past us, anxious to add their weight to the fury.

"I see it Father," she says. "There is no place we can flee. No safety in a storm."

"Yes. Hope is all but lost," I say. A trumpet trills in the distance, triggering memories of events to come.

There is a light upon the battlefield, a flame as bright as the sun, as bright as the very fires of creation. Wielded in the hand of a champion, it hovers over our heads, drawing the enemy's eyes away from their dark tasks. As we gaze at it The

Sword twists, turning from straight to curved, a meandering river of blood, dark red and blistered like a festering wound. It glistens, moist and sticky, swinging above the heads of my enemies, a Sword of Fire with the power to deliver God's justice with every blow.

A cruel blow it is, the justice swift that day. As The Sword touches my foes they are transformed. The dark, red light of The Sword sticks to their bodies, attaching itself and spreading across their skin with that same festering-red sickness. Some of them hunch over, their bodies twisting in agony as limbs reform into animal shapes and heads erupt with bumps and horns. The air is filled with the sound of pain, screams of agony and torment, a bitter blend of animal and angel.

This, my daughter sees with me, a fate worse than death reflected through my eyes. What can be worse than horrible, unimaginable disfigurement? Add eternal life, perhaps, for if angels can die, demons can only hope to.

The battle continues to rage, my daughter to cling ever tighter to my robe. Through my visions we see an arm lopped off by The Sword. It falls to the ground and twists into a slug-like creature, taking on a life all its own. Meanwhile its former master mutates into a gelatinous mass of flesh pockmarked with blemishes and sores. Others around him, touched by The Sword, drop to the ground becoming unrecognizable shapes, strange creatures that defy description. As these hapless beings change, there is a sound from them like bones being crushed in a gristmill. These new sounds join the cacophony of battle around us, chorused by wails unlike any I have heard or ever will hear again. It is the lament of lost form and presence.

I turn and face one of these devils. He is screaming at me, the nails on his fingers elongated like sharp talons now. He claws at his face as if it were a mask he would hope to remove, but it is obvious that it will not come off. This masquerade will never end, and the deep, bleeding claw marks he is inflicting on himself do not improve things.

"You're right," my daughter says hoarsely, turning away from me as if I were a poisoned well. "There are things worse than death."

I stare down, closing myself off from her. I try to step away but she grabs my arm as if to comfort me. I am accustomed to worshiping the Almighty, not asking for favors, but I pray to God for a respite, to please take these visions away, for her sake if for no other. Even as I think these words, I realize I have asked God this favor before, but for whatever reason the visions remain.

She screams, her piercing cry drowning out everything. I close my eyes and the sounds disappear. When I open them again, we are back in my garden.

It was unintentional on her part, her question as innocent as rain when it wets the flowers, but she seems to possess her mother's ability to expose what we hide within ourselves. This ability appears to be getting stronger in her as she grows older, developing like any muscle would when it is exercised. I suspect it is her angel power. Unlike my wife she is young and cannot yet control it.

I place my hand over hers, saying, "I am all right now."

She smiles. "Me, too."

"The visions are gone for the moment," I say. "When they pass I am often left with a strange emotion. Emptiness, loss, despair, I can't quite describe it but I am in such a state now."

"I know," she says. I wonder if, like her mother, she can sense my feelings. "Tell me more," she says.

"I am fascinated with the phrase fallen comrade," I say, my mind still blurred. "I wonder if the phrase is an Earthly reflection of that Heavenly battle waged so long ago, for as you surmise, that is what we have been seeing. I was there when it started. I saw the first angels fall."

I pull myself together and focus. These are things I did not wish upon her, yet now that they are exposed, how can I hope to hide them again? I cannot take back what she has seen in me, all I can do is help her to understand me.

"You still have not answered my question," she says. "Have you ever seen an angel die?"

"No," I say. "Angels are immortal, at least that is what I believe."

After a pause of silence, she asks, "What about me?"

"What do you mean?" I ask. "What about you?"

"Can I die?"

"You are an angel." I tell her, comforting her with logic. "How can you die?" I say, but I do not know for certain. I have my doubts. I don't know if angels can die. There are many who disappeared during that time, many I have never seen again. Does that mean they are dead?

"Unlike you, Father, I am not an angel that God created," she says. "I am the child of you and Mother."

"What does that have to do with anything?" I ask.

"Maybe I don't have the powers that you and Mother have," she says. "Maybe I'm not immortal."

"Does it matter?" I ask, grabbing her up in my arms. I am sad, wondering how we have come to this in our discussion. "You are much too young to be thinking of death." I try to move her away from such dismal thoughts.

She smiles, and I am glad I can distract her. I do not want her to grow up so quickly, despite her impatience. I raise her high above my head and spread my wings, threatening to fly away with her. She giggles like the excited child she should be, and the heaviness is lifted from us for the moment.

3. Daddy Tell Me a Story

The moment is fleeting, and sadness descends upon her again like a shroud covering a lifeless, Earth-bound body. I sense the change in her and gently set her down.

"How can that happen?" she asks.

"What?" I ask.

"Angels fighting angels, brothers and sisters locked in combat with each other?"

"I don't know," I say.

"There must have been great discord in Heaven," she says, her mind grasping at answers again.

"There was," I say.

"You must tell me about it," she says. "How can there be hope for peace on Earth when none can be found in Heaven?"

"There is peace here," I say. "Can't you feel it? Besides, that battle was long ago, back around the time God created Man."

"Did Man cause the fight?" she asks. "Mankind is definitely capable of it."

"Man certainly was an issue in the fight, at least that is what Satan would have you believe. But Man was young and innocent back then, a simple creature destined for life in the Garden of Eden. They were like children, not even aware of the events in Heaven at the time. I don't think the blame can be laid upon their shoulders."

"Tell me about the fight," she demands. "How could such a thing happen? I still don't understand it."

"I'm not sure I understand it myself," I say.

"Then tell me what you do know," she pleads with me.

"But you already know the story," I say, trying to shake her free of this morbid subject.

"Oh, yes, you've told me the story," she says. "But you haven't told me the truth."

"But I have!" I say.

She stares into my eyes and I feel ill again. "You've told me a story all right," she says. "A children's story. I know all about Michael and his flaming Sword, but I never pictured it like that. I have overheard you and Mother discussing events from those times. I know the story, a child's story, a watered down version of history made for bedtime. Now tell me the story, the real one, or let me into your mind so I can see more of it for myself."

I am like a volcano waiting to explode. Her words hang there, molten in my head.

"Why would angels fight each other?" she asks. "Tell me, please, and not the fairy tale version of the story, the real thing."

I hesitate. "Some other time," I say. "I do not like having these memories stirred, least of all dwelling upon them." I can feel them at the dull edge of my perception, trying to come out of hiding again.

"Sometimes when you talk about things, they get better," she says, coaxing me. I feel her angel powers probing me, trying to turn me inside out.

4. History Repeats Itself

"To understand history you must understand the minds of the people at the time. History is not just events, it is the evolution of ideas, and the two are interrelated. The war in Heaven, like many other wars, was over ideology and a difference in beliefs."

"You once told me that God withheld Grace from some of the angels, and this made them fall," she says.

"Yes. So goes the legend," I say. "But that is a simple explanation, one more suited for a child."

She understands what I mean. The scrunch lines on her face ripple like waves, evidence of the thoughts churning deep within her.

"Where did the Sword of Fire come from?" she asks.

"God gave Michael that Sword, created in some unknown forge. He told Michael to use it to protect

Mankind. Although there was a time when I saw The Sword used against Man."

"What happened?" she asks.

"After that ancient battle, Lucifer and the Downcasts knew they would never return. The walls of Heaven were strengthened to protect the security of this, the ultimate Fortress of Goodness. The Firmament became littered with filters and barriers to keep the Fallen Ones away. It also became a limbo that sometimes traps uncertain souls in their journey to find Heaven."

I draw a breath and continue. "With these limitations, Lucifer plotted to get back at God. He made evil his goodness and his goal, treating it as if it were his holy mission. His first act after his expulsion was to tempt Man, exposing the flaw in God's Creation. God was hurt, and in anger He cast Man out of His Garden of Eden, sending Michael with his flaming Sword to chase Adam and Eve away."

"Where did they go?" she asks.

"Wandering somewhere East of Eden, in a land that forced hardship and work upon them. It was what God decreed, fitting because Man had been disobedient and because he wanted the knowledge of the forbidden tree. The knowledge came with a price."

There are waves of thought across her face again. "God knew about all this?" she asks.

"What do you think?" I ask.

I see her mind at work, churning up thoughts that I myself have struggled with. Perhaps she will come up with better answers, if any at all.

"Can we change the subject?" she asks.

"Of course."

"When are you going to take me to Earth again?" she asks.

This is another debate we have. I doubt Earth could present her with any more horror than she has just seen through me. This is what I tell myself, but I am wrong. Our last visit was a nightmare. Why she would wish to return is beyond me, but I can see the draw. God has told us to help and serve Mankind and many of us are fascinated with Earth. Angels flex their wings and reach their full potential there.

They are needed. Through service we fulfill our destiny, but it is a harsh environment. As a parent I want to protect her as long as possible. The burden is great for a spirit so young, and it could harm her development. Yet she longs to see the Earth again.

"Soon, my child," I say, putting her off.

"You said that the last time I asked. Please tell me when we can go."

"Soon." I know I will have to take her again one day. Patience may be a virtue, but I fear what could happen to her if I take her below the Firmament. Earth is the middle ground, and I am known as a Neutral Angel, marked and hunted by the Fallen Ones.

This is another secret I have kept from her. What is one more stone in my hidden pile of rocks?

"How soon?" she whines.

I blurt out my anxiety. "Didn't you get enough of Earth last time?"

5. I Recall Our Last Trip to Earth

She twists away from me and I sense her frustration.

"You do remember the last time," I say.

"I'd rather not," she says. Her arms fold across her chest as she turns away.

"They were harsh lessons," I say. "We started with the best of intentions. It was not long ago, you must remember. We had a discussion about prayer as we descended through the Firmament."

"I remember!" she says, her voice firm and hard as she turns back to face me. Her eyes narrow and she stares at me through harsh slits. She opens her arms to reveal a new ability to me. Her heart glows and emits a beam of bright light that solidifies into miniature versions of our selves in front of her. They float through clouds, drifting down through layers of Firmament as they descend toward Earth.

I am mesmerized. There is a tug and I begin to fall forward into this tiny scene until it grows and surrounds me. I feel the pressure on my face, the liquid thickness of the Firmament swirling past us. I hear amplified sounds, the twisted acoustics that are characteristic of this environment. We hold hands and we begin to again experience the events of that fateful day.

"What is that noise, Father?" she asks.

"It is the sound of prayers," I explain to her.

"But it's so loud," she says, reaching towards her ears.

"We are passing through the medium between that which lies above the Firmament and below. Sound, especially the sound of prayers, is amplified by this medium, much the way water will amplify sounds when we immerse ourselves in it."

"Do all prayers travel this path?" she asks.

"Some bounce right back to Earth and never get this far," I say. *"God does not need to hear all prayers. The Firmament acts almost like a filter. Prayers with particular vibrations bounce back,*

such as prayers for world peace, for the health of a loved one, or for light and knowledge. These prayers are amplified and made more powerful. They have a saying on Earth that God helps those who help themselves. This is one way that this power becomes manifest. When the prayers bounce back the high vibration prayers become brighter and stronger. Prayers for health, for example, return to find the loved ones they are intended for, surrounding them with a healing energy. It vitalizes them with the combined power of God's love and prayer."

"How can that be?" she asks.

"God lives in all men's hearts, whether they sense it or not," I explain. "That is the true source of power. When the intention is pure, it causes a perfect reflection, a true image of the purpose of the prayer. The prayer always finds its destination."

"What if, like you said, it is a prayer for world peace?" she asks. "A prayer like that doesn't have a particular destination. What happens when it reflects back towards the Earth?"

"When it hits this filter, it explodes like a star and rains back upon the Earth, scattering like seeds in the wind. Wherever the pieces fall, positive effects are felt."

"So why isn't the Earth all healed and happy?" she asks. "It seems like everyone would be happy if this were the case."

"It would be if everyone wanted world peace," I say. "Don't worry, there will be world peace one day, when men find God in their hearts and offer up more selfless prayers."

"And what about the other prayers?" she asks. "You said other kinds of prayers are bounced back. What are these bouncing prayers?"

"Selfish prayers," I say. "These prayers actually go nowhere. These are low vibration prayers for money, fame, Earthly things. Good people work hard for their dreams and give prayers of thanks, but these selfish prayers are different. They bounce back and fall to Earth, unfulfilled, settling like dust at the feet of the petitioners."

She nods in understanding as I continue. "Sometimes they can come true, but often in horrific ways. For example, a man prays for money, imagining he is getting a large sum. He prays and prays, creating strong thought forms that act to solidify his wishes. One day he cuts his hands off in milling machine, only to find that he is unable to hold the check for the large sum of money that the *insurance company sends him as a settlement for the accident. Worse, the money goes not for his imagined luxuries, but for the necessities of his new life."*

"Then there are these kinds of prayers, the type we are hearing now, those that penetrate the barrier between Heaven and Earth." I stretch out my free hand and grab the sound wave. The prayer becomes tangible, solidifying like a golden rope in my grasp. "Hold on to me," I say. She squeezes my hand and I grip it tight. "This prayer is a desperate call for help. See how easily it becomes solid?"

"How could you tell it was important?" she asks.

"By its color," I say. "The more urgent the prayer, the brighter it's color."

"What makes these prayers special?" she asks.

"I really don't know," I answer. "But somehow they have the power to reach the very ears of God. This one we are holding is something important. When an angel sees or feels a prayer like this, it has to be investigated."

There is a tug from the prayer we are holding, pulling us with a sense of urgency. "Hold on," I say. "The cry has become even stronger. We'll be on Earth soon, riding on a prayer."

"What will we do when we get there?" she asks.

"It will be time to go to work," I say.

6. A Prayer Answered

We break through the Firmament and into the sky above the Earth. There are many angels emerging from the clouds, all guided by prayers that lead to the hearts of the callers. An airplane thunders below us where they converge. The plane lurches and dips low into the sky, as if to fall, but guided instead with deadly purpose.

"Oh, no," she cries, realizing what I have already seen. The plane is headed towards a building, one of two tall towers of glass standing beside the waters of a great city. I follow the string of the prayer I hold, realizing that she has let go of my hand and found a prayer of her own to follow.

Inside the plane people are crying. A man dark with evil intent faces terrified passengers. A limp body lies in a pool of blood blocking the aisle before him. The same blood stains a box cutter gripped firmly in his right hand. "You may use your cell phones now if you like," he says in a calm voice.

My prayer leads to a woman. Beside her is a small child. She looks at the child, a tear in her eye, but he does not look back at her. He stares out the window. On the wing I see my daughter smiling. The child laughs and she beckons him as if inviting him to play. The woman looks out the window and I think she can see my little angel too. She mutters another prayer to God and I whisper in her ear, "Be not afraid, for I am with you. God has sent an angel to guide you home."

At that moment the plane crashes into the building and fire erupts all about us. Her spirit is jarred loose, knocked free of the flames. She holds her child in her arms, clinging to what she can, but he is already becoming ethereal. His little body is gone, and like a butterfly freed from life as a caterpillar, he suddenly emerges with full wings. So it is with those who die in innocence. The wings spread apart, and now he is holding his mother aloft. I help him by cradling her body in my powerful arms, my daughter beside me. All around us we see angels doing the same, holding beings aloft in their arms.

"It's beautiful," the woman says, as if seeing us for the first time.

"Yes, it is," I reply. I did not want her to look down and see the tragedy unfolding before us. Flames begin to blacken the sky as the tower burns, but I hold her firm. I point out the line of prayer that led us to her. It stretches from her heart to a light in the distant sky, an iridescent rainbow of hope.

"Look, Mommy," says the little boy. "I see God."

"Yes. Now you must go to Him," I say softly. "Hold onto this prayer and it will guide you to Him." The golden cord tugs at her heart, pulling her towards the Firmament above. "Go," I say. "Paradise waits for you. Rest and peace after a lifetime of pain and Earthly suffering."

"Will you be there too?" the little boy asks, turning to my daughter.

"In a little while," she says.

"Will you play with me?" he asks her.

"Of course," she smiles. "But you must hurry. You and your Mom must hurry. Follow your prayers, for they have been answered," she says.

Pride may be a sin, but I could not have been more proud of her at that moment. All regrets I had about bringing her suddenly disappeared. Celestial work and acts of kindness are what angels do after all.

We watch for a moment as the child and his mother are drawn away from us on gossamer threads, pulled back to the source of all life. Many other souls recede into the distance, pulled by threads that weave in and around each other into a tapestry made from pure love.

We do not have time to enjoy it anymore, for below us a scene of great tragedy unfolds. More angels appear, God's own rescue workers. Around the burning building men and women rush about. Some have angels at their sides, guiding them to unseen places. Others hold back the morass of humanity that rushes forward to help. I quickly lose sight of my daughter, for she has fallen to Earth, speeding towards a group of children who are evacuating a nearby school. Before I can react a second plane appears, flying low and ominous in the sky. Anxious fingers point, and it becomes all too clear what is about to happen. More flames erupt as the airplane plunges into the second tower. Cries and prayers also erupt, a fountain of petitions, blessings, and hopes that bounce off the Firmament and shower down upon the writhing mass of humanity like a torrent of cooling water.

A golden stairway suddenly drops from the shower of prayers, reaching from the clouds to settle gently beside the collapsing pile of rubble. I have seen Jacob's ladder only a few times in my long lifetime and service as an angel, but never like this. The smoke coils about it, but it is transparent, as if floating in another dimension. The rails glow with golden light, and each stair shimmers like the sun reflected in a clear pool. At the base of the stairs, angels stand, reaching out to souls stumbling towards salvation. "This way, please," they say gently, wrapping them in golden cloaks as they step upon the staircase.

"But I was going down the stairs," I hear one say in astonishment. "I was escaping the building. The stairs were going downward!"

"Yes, they were," the angel says softly. "And now they lead up. Up and into the light."

"It's a miracle," the soul cries.

"Yes, it is," says the angel.

I look in another direction and see a procession of evil. For these poor souls the stairs continue to lead down. The fires never stop and Satan's equivalent to Jacob's ladder, if there can be such a thing, leads them deep into the darkness beneath the Earth. The fire that eats the last remnants of the collapsed buildings burns on their flesh. The flames will never go out and they are prodded onward by demons who appear from crevices and shadows within the rubble.

"What are those, Father?" my daughter asks.

"The Fallen Ones," I say.

Upon hearing my voice, a demon turns to look at me. I recognize in his eyes one who I called friend so long ago, long before the separation of Heaven and Hell. Instead of a cloak of white and wings of golden feathers, his skin is scabbous and blotched, his wings dark nubs that have atrophied like unharvested fruit rotting on the vine. I sense both sadness and a sense of purpose in his eyes, a purpose equal to my own.

"Tartaruch," I say, remembering his name.

He sneers at me, continuing to prod his victims with a rusty spear. "Get away," he warns. "I don't have time for your righteous indignation."

"Why do you do it?" I ask.

"It's my job," he says. "I am set over punishments. These Barons of Wall Street knew well what awaited them in the afterlife. They had their chances at humanity, some of them many times over. I'm here to see they get their just rewards." He brandishes his weapon and narrows his eyes. "Now get away before I decide to collect the reward on your hide."

I watch him work, a smile on his lips as he carries out his heinous tasks. I know Lucifer awaits these souls with anxious arms, taking joy in what he keeps from God, souls the Divine has created from the light of His celestial love. I imagine the perverse pleasure Satan gets from this act and the twisted satisfaction he gains by denying everlasting light to the condemned.

Then there is the torture, the pleasure that the Fallen Ones derive by inflicting endless pain. By doing this, do they escape their own pain? I do not know what goes on in Hell, but I can imagine the suffering. I wonder what becomes of the mote of God that lives on in the hearts of men. Is there hope in Hell or has Satan found a way to mine these jewels for his own enjoyment.

Then I see him, the Devil himself, standing beside the man from the plane who had only recently held a bloodied box cutter in his hands. Lucifer stares at me. He has an awareness that, though not omniscient, is strong and alert. He smiles, nodding to me. His eyes still upon me, he whispers into the man's ear, "This way," pointing downward. "Your reward awaits you, my friend. Ten thousand virgins, their tongues burning with desire for your flesh." His smile widens as the man begins to descend the fiery staircase. He turns back to smile and Satan shimmers, his image shifting. The man stares back, now seeing the devil as he was taught by the priests of his own religion.

Tartaruch steps forward to lead him away. "He's special," rasps Lucifer. "Something about him I like. Take him to my trophy room." They join the procession, demons prodding them on into a gauntlet of pain. Lucifer comes to my side. "Once again we meet upon the battlefield of Earth to reap our spoils."

I am not afraid, and I resist the urge to become his antonym, staying focused upon my own philosophy of neutrality and the Middle Way. "Yes, my old friend," I say softly, meeting not as adversaries in battle, but as true friends. He sees into my heart and knows, like God, what I am thinking. He knows at that moment that I still love him, that true to God's wishes, it is what I feel for him above all. There is no sadness, only love, the love of finding a long lost brother and wanting to welcome him home.

"I don't need your love," he spits.

"I can't help it," I say.

"I know you can't," he replies, his eyes reflecting hatred where I once found love.

"I miss you," I say.

He has no retort for that. I can only imagine what he is thinking, weighing his loss of Heaven against the pain of Hell. There is a commotion behind him and he sneers at me and retreats, turning to shout for his men to grab more souls and pull them unwillingly down into his domain. About me I look at the scene of destruction, seeing rescue workers and bystanders fight for life, unaware that in the same space and time a fight for death is also underway.

Several of the Fallen Ones rush forward, shielding their eyes from the light. Inspired by the presence of their leader, they run towards the golden staircase. Before hostility can begin, I see Michael descend the staircase, his hands wrapped around a flaming sword that glows with power. Souls ascending the staircase quickly scramble to the side rails, making way for the mighty Archangel. Angels near the ground hasten, moving those destined for Heaven's gate quickly toward the staircase. Devils confront them and the angels form a circle of protection around them. My heart sinks as I see the old lines drawn, good and evil squaring off once again for a battle as old as time.

Satan does not waste an instant. Upon seeing Michael, he reaches into the pit and pulls out his own fantastic weapon, something I had not seen before. It is a stout staff, forked at one end, crackling with the same spark as the mythic Sword of Fire. With it he swipes at the defending angels' feet, pushing them aside like broken timbers.

Michael moves quickly now, opening his wings and flying off the staircase. With his Sword thrust forward he directs it between Satan and the angels, catching the fork amid the tines. The Earth shakes with the power, and at that moment, the second tower collapses. Smoke and debris are everywhere. In the center of that mass, as the smoke clears, I see Michael and Lucifer locked in battle. Fire dances off The Sword and lightning strikes in all directions. People flee, instinctively knowing that more than glass and steel are breaking. The very fabric of time is being ripped once again.

My daughter runs behind me, hiding at my back. I sweep her up, carrying her away from all this to a place of safety.

"Why don't you help them, Father?" she asks, and sadness fills me to tears. Before I can answer her, I

notice the Ladder becoming unstable. "Quickly," I say to her. "There are souls at stake."

Several angels form a line and protect the retreating spirits of the dead while demons hiss and claw at them. The Earth shakes again as Michael and Lucifer strike at each other with their mighty weapons. Where is God, I wonder, but I know He is in Heaven, tending to His own business, the business of saving souls, welcoming them and warming them with love after a lifetime of unrest and tragedy. The other end of this staircase is just as busy as this end, cluttered with confusion.

Another crack as Lucifer and Michael fight without regard to those around them. The pits of Hell open wider, swallowing pieces of the buildings and more souls of the damned. The ladder becomes choked with traffic. Both the living and the dead cry out in pain but there is no peace to be found here.

My child clings to my robe and I regret bringing her here. "Is it always like this?" she asks, terrified at what she is seeing.

"Not always," I say. "But it is time for us to retreat."

"But I don't want to leave," she says.

"You must," I say. "It is no longer safe for you here."

"But what about them," she says, indicating the souls, both living and dead, struggling to cope with this nightmare.

"They will be all right," I say. "Look!" I point skyward. The air is filled with angels and Heavenly hosts descending from upon high. Willful to the Word of God, the reserves have been called up. The mightiest Archangels fall into line, quickly attacking the demons that hold unwilling souls in their grasp. Shouts erupt and weapons clang, souls scream and scurry toward the safety of the Ladder.

Demons pour up from the pits, exploding like a geyser of oil from a fresh derrick. They come from everywhere, the debris, the smoke in the air, the cracks in the pavement, even from the hearts of some men.

I take my daughter away from all this, back through the Firmament and upwards into Heaven. As we clear the filter, I see several small children with her, gripped tightly in her hands. As I had rescued her, so had she managed to rescue them.

I look over at her and she is smiling. The images fade and we are back in our garden, freed from the horrors of that day. Her heart glows gently as the beam of light that began this adventure returns to its source.

I have a new, deeper appreciation of the events and the roles we played. Who says we cannot learn from our children?

7. Agape

"How long have you had this power over the past?" I ask.

"I don't know," she says. "Not long."

"You are growing up fast," I remark, and she smiles. "Do you really want to go back to Earth?" I ask her. "Even after your last experience?"

"More than ever," she says.

"I don't see why," I say. "What fascinates you most about that trip?"

Her face scrunches again. "The way you confronted Satan," she says.

I am surprised by this answer and demand more details. "Why that? Was nothing else interesting? Jacob's Ladder? Prayer? Rescuing children? You even saw battle, not my second hand visions. Help me understand."

"I know that you are a Neutral Angel. I have heard you and Mother say that often. But I didn't know what that meant until I saw how you treated Satan and the Fallen Ones that day."

"What did I do?" I ask.

"You... loved him," she says. "While other angels attacked him and his horde, you showed them love."

"Fighting is useless," I say. "Evil cannot be eliminated in the world, only resisted from within. Besides, I know no other way. To love your enemy, to truly love your enemy, is the ultimate form of spiritual love. Satan once called me a caricature of God, and in that respect perhaps I am a caricature, but for me, and for any true Angel of God, there is no other form of love."

She smiles.

"You were born of that love," I tell her. "God has blessed me with child. A rare form of Angelic agape joined your Mother and I in bliss to bring about new life. That is how you came into being."

"Can all angels have children?"

"I don't know," I answer. "Perhaps they can, but child angels are rare. I believe they happen only to those who share a special bond."

"Love?" she asks. Her scrunch is different now, her marble face contoured in confusion. Perhaps questions about love weigh just as deep with young angels as they do with their earthly counterparts. Indeed, the Daughters of Men, all mankind for that matter, seem to struggle with love.

"Of course I mean love," I say. "There is no stronger bond, and your mother and I are bonded as no other. We draw strength from one another."

"I see how you are with each other," she says. "When you embrace, especially after being apart for some time, you seem to fuse together as you hold each other. A bright light forms and the two of you retreat into a bubble of love."

"A good description of it," I say.

"Is that passion?" she asks.

"Love takes many forms," I explain. "Do not attempt to put a label on it or try to describe it in words. Love is very personal. We use words to communicate the broader categories of love. For example, what we have been talking about is compassion, which is quite different from passion."

"What's the difference?"

"Passion is a zeal, enthusiasm that can border on obsession. You can have a passion for art, for life, and even for another being. Thus, passion is often used to describe the depth of love felt between two people. But passion can be selfish and it has earthly limits. Compassion, on the other hand, is more like empathy. It involves a spiritual awareness of the other person and is less focused on the self. Lucifer has experienced both sides of this love, passion being one of the tricks in his arsenal. Often Earthly love brings only temporary bliss, and the lovers seem to sense this. Whatever sustains love, it is this force that compels me to embrace Lucifer when I see him. Compassion is, in my opinion, a better form of love to practice."

"Is that what you and Mother share?"

"Partly," I say. "I can only say we share something special. As I said, love is deeply personal, and your mother and I have bonded over many things on many levels."

"And your love for Lucifer?" she asks. "It seems to go deeper than that, too. I daresay you love him as much as you do Mother."

Again she is probing me with her angelic powers. Her face is smooth now, her eyes deep and focused.

I can deny her the truth no longer. The words crawl out of my heart before I can rescind them. "Lucifer is my brother," I say.

"Like all angels are brothers?" she asks.

"No," I say. "Lucifer is my brother. Your Uncle, born at my side and raised together by the same Father. He is your true Uncle and, next to you and Mother, my closest relative."

8. Lucifer, My Brother

"We called him Son of the Morning Star. Of all God's angels he was the most handsome, the most beautiful. Even after his fall he did not lose that quality. Mankind holds some fascination for him, for he is seductive. I find it easy to love and admire him," I say, adding, "Despite our differences."

"Uncle Lucifer," she says, her voice childlike, putting the words together for the first time.

"He was God's favorite, and who wouldn't want to be seen with God's favorite?" I say. "Perhaps he made God think about things, too, which might be why He kept Lucifer close, for nobody loved God more than my brother, which is his pain now. I know his story is tainted with arrogance, and maybe that was something added as the tale was told and retold, but in the beginning there truly was no angel that loved and served God more than Lucifer.

"This, I believe, is the source of the greatest pain and the greatest suffering in his punishment. To be separated from the one you truly love is the most horrible fate I can imagine. Many times have I seen the suffering caused on Earth by two people who love each other and for one reason or another, they separate. Earthly love is but a reflection of God's love, and so I cannot imagine what Satan must now feel, but I know that his agony must be the very source of the fires of Hell.

"As brothers, we spoke often, probably because I am a good listener. I can't say when I first detected discord in him, but it became evident that he was not content."

9. The Origin of Angels

"Is it true God created us first?" she asks me.

"Angels?" I answer. "Yes."

"Before He created Mankind?"

"Yes," I answer again. "You know that."

"Why did we come first? Why angels?" she asks.

I pause to think. "I don't know. Only God knows that."

"Are people better than angels?"

"No, just different. All God's creatures are different. Even within our family we are all different."

"Yes, but how are people different?" she asks.

"They have free will," I explain.

"But we all have free will."

"True, true," I say, thinking. "Angels serve a higher purpose."

"Than Man?" she asks.

"We are closer to God," I say.

"And farther from evil," she says. "It's easy for us here in Heaven."

"Yes," I say. "God's grace keeps us safe and maintains peace here in Heaven. Souls can rest here free of the temptation and suffering they endured through life."

"Free of evil," she says.

10. Free?

"What is evil, Father?"

She asks a fundamental question. Her mind is changing, reaching for the conscience she needs to navigate adulthood. I wonder if I have been gone too much lately, spending too much time on Earth. It's not just that the world population has increased, but Earth is a busy place these days. She is my child, and I can see her need for knowledge and guidance. Her innocence in that question is refreshing, but how do I answer her? Thirteen going on twenty and at this moment she is again thirteen to me.

"Hold on to that innocence," I say to her, placing my hand on her cheek. I think back into the events of my life and I cannot remember my own innocence. I can only have that through her. Am I selfish to keep her from aging?

She is impatient and asks again. "What is evil? Can't you tell me, Father?"

"It is hard to explain. You need to grow up some more before I can explain it to you." I say these words realizing that I am again giving her a simple answer. Of course she is not satisfied.

"When?" she asks.

"When you grow up."

I see the disappointment in her. "That may take forever," she says.

I laugh. "We have all of eternity."

"How old are you?" she asks.

"Old enough to know that such questions are not polite to ask," I say.

"I know you are very old," she says in a tone that I might describe as precocious were she an Earth child. "You were there in the beginning, weren't you?"

"Yes. Yes, I was", I confess. "But you know that already. I have told you that story."

It has been a long time since I have told her that story, but she has a good memory. "I know how God created the Heavens and the Earth. And then He created evil."

"God did not create evil," I correct her. "Where did you hear that?"

"God created Lucifer, didn't He? Isn't Lucifer the father of all evil? If God created him, then didn't He create evil to begin with?" she asks.

She is a clever child, and twenty again, her adult mind probing me for weaknesses in my logic. "When did you start thinking such things? Whom have you been talking to?" I ask.

"A friend of mine," she says. "Iblis."

"I don't want you talking to Iblis anymore."

"But you just said we have free will."

Child logic. It is the same in Heaven as it is on Earth. "Yes. But only when you get older. You need more experience as an adult."

"Then take me to Earth again."

"Since when have you become so demanding?" I ask.

"Since I have this hunger to know what things are like there," she pleads. "Is it true that, on Earth, there is evil everywhere?"

"And what is this interest in evil?" I ask, surprised now. "It's not a healthy interest."

"I just want to know, Father," she says.

I can't fault her that. How can you recognize evil if you never confront it? There is a universal fascination with evil. At times I stare into it, seeing my own reflection as if looking into a black pool. I do not wish to do evil, and because of that my actions guide my purpose. But I ponder its purpose in the scheme of things.

"You and Uncle Lucifer were good friends before the Fall, weren't you?" she says. "You almost followed him into Hell."

"Did Iblis tell you that?" I ask.

"No," she says. "Mother did."

I consider it for a moment. If my wife thinks she is ready for such information, who am I to question?

"In the Beginning, your Uncle and I were inseparable. Brothers united, Archangels of the innermost order, bound by service to God. We worked closely together. Those were glorious days. We were tasked with dangerous missions essential to the holy order that kept Heaven intact and running smoothly. But most of all, like true brothers, we enjoyed each other's company. He made me think, although I do not know where he got his ideas."

I am silent, lost in thought. She jars me with her words. "You reminiscence too much Father," she says.

"Perhaps," I say, but I know she is right. I focus on the present. "You must be wary of temptation," I tell her. "It is true that you have free will, and no one can change that. But you must always make up your own mind about things and choose your own path."

"Yes, Father," she says.

"Most of all you must think." I explain to her. "Many, including the Devil, will try to trick you into making a wrong decision. That's why it is very important that you think for yourself. If you need help making a decision, talk to someone you trust, but always, *always* think for yourself."

She reflects silently for a while. Her face is sad and she looks at me through tear filled eyes.

"What is it, my little angel?" I ask.

"The visions." Surely there are tears in her eyes now. They glisten like stars against a dark sky. "A gift from your brother, you said. That can only mean that Satan..."

The words hang there on the edge of a precipice. I push her over, tumbling her from a place to which she can never return. "Your Uncle," I say, but she has no words and neither do I.

The silence of the still heart cannot be disturbed. Time passes slowly and without comment. Finally she asks, "Will you tell me the story of the Sword of Fire again? The real story of your past? I want to know our family history."

She has a pointed desire. There will be no satisfaction until she hears it, and there will be no rest for me if I do not yield. Her mother is the same way. "Yes, I will tell you," I say, giving in to the inevitable. "It is a long story."

"We have all of eternity," she says.

11.Something Different

"How about your power?" I ask. "Can't you just tap into my mind and replay my past?"

"I tried before," she says. "It doesn't seem to work that way. I can summon up anything in my own past, but not much beyond that. Your history remains personal and hidden from me."

"Oh," I say.

"But we could try," she says.

"What do you suggest?" I ask.

"Maybe if we get comfortable and you open yourself up to me."

She guides me to a celestial hammock in a corner of our garden and we lay down among the stars. She positions herself over my stomach and we recline much as we did when she was younger. My mind slips back to those days when we shared each other's thoughts. Her mother was often gone, one of many angels in demand, doing God's work on Earth. I remember what it was like spending time with her as a baby.

"Hmmm," I mutter a gentle sound. The humming soothes my heart while I struggle with a difficult decision. "Are you prepared for anything?" I ask, watching her nod all too quickly. Her marble face is serious, trying to look anything but child-like. "My past is full of turmoil. I will open myself up to your probing, but you must remain silent until I am finished presenting it to you."

"How will I know when we are finished?" she asks.

"You will know. If not, I will tell you," I say. "Let us begin."

I take a deep breath. Thoughts eddy in my consciousness. I drift in and out of scenes from my past: personal battles, life with my brother, how I met my wife, adventures we shared. They bubble to the surface of my consciousness and burst into my thoughts. I see them discretely and with great clarity, an array of moments that make up my life.

My daughter squeezes my hand and I realize she is with me in my thoughts. My past floats like soap bubbles in a breeze before us. I see events from my life swirling on their surfaces reflected in oily rainbow colors. She smiles and we are pulled towards these bubbles. As they burst around us thoughts rain down on our skin opening up visions of my world and what it once was like.

12. The Father of All Lawyers

The first bubble pulls us into one of the many conversations I had with Lucifer. My mind presents the story like any other, starting with details that set the stage for the drama to come. Conversations with my brother were always interesting, and the one we now find ourselves in is typical. He has a way with words. This bubble has all the particulars, encapsulated in thoughts that easily open before us. It is in such conversations that I first sensed the seeds of discord.

"I am less than I can be," he says to me.

"What makes you say that?" I ask him. *"How can you be less than what you are?"*

"I work hard for the Glory of God," he says. *"At times I feel I can do more. Do you ever feel like that?"*

"No. I can't say that I do," I say.

"God is all-seeing," he intones. "All-knowing."

"Yes," I reply.

"He will never die."

"Never," I say.

He looks towards the golden office at the end of the hall, then turns his head sadly towards the floor. "I will never be in charge."

Ambition. Sometimes I think it was Lucifer who taught humanity this concept. I turn to speak to him and we are no longer in an office, but suddenly on a ship. On this ship Lucifer is both Captain and navigator, steering the ship with a big wheel as he looks off into the distance. This is one of his angel powers, the ability to change the environment to shape his desires. In all respects the ship is solid, a stout wooden sailing vessel. The sea beneath it rolls gently as we sail across the waves. Invisible forces move lines and set sails, for there is no crew, only myself and Lucifer. Where is he taking me with this conversation?

"Why would you want to be in charge?" I ask.

"Come now," he says. "Have you never thought that you could be more than an angel?"

"Why should I? This is what I was created to be. I'm happy being an angel. The only way I could be more is if God wanted me to be more. All that I am is by the grace of God."

"Then why should I feel different?" he asks.

"You're an important Angel, Lucifer. Everyone looks up to you."

"Yes, they do. But they look to God first."

"As it should be," I say.

He looks over at me from the side, his eyes slick and wistful. "Not all of the angels look to God first," he says. His words hold a strange taste for me. They leave something unsettled on my palate.

"I didn't see you at adoration this morning," he says, changing the subject.

"I wasn't there," I answer. "What did I miss?"

"Only God, the Almighty Himself, bestowing upon me yet another blessing."

"Were you wearing your jewel encrusted bodice again?" I ask, goading him on.

"Still wearing it," he says, bearing his cloak open before me. From beneath it comes such a light, a beautiful, soft palate of colors. I swear I can hear music in that color. The light shines out like a ray of love, and I am caught up in it. I just want to gaze upon it and enjoy the feeling of peace and warmth that is upon me.

And then he closes his cloak, and I am pushed outside again.

13. Pain in Heaven

"God is lucky to have you to help Him run things," I say.

"Yes," agrees Lucifer. *"He trusts me more and more with His affairs."*

"You do a good job," I say.

"I seem to have a better eye for the details," he says. *"He can only see the big picture, but there are always details to attend to. Do you know what would happen if I did not plan Adoration properly? What if I had not reorganized the Heavenly Choir? Have you noticed the difference in the sound lately?"* He pauses, and I hear the Choir, ethereal and light, a blend of voices both full and hollow, mixing to a feeling of perfection in my heart. The sound is a constant foundation upon which Heaven rests.

There is so much peace in Heaven. I enjoy it wherever I can find it. But peace is somehow foreign to my brother.

"Why do I feel like I can do a better job?" he asks. "If I were in charge of Heaven there would be more purpose to existence than just Worship and Adoration."

"But I like Adoration," I say. "Besides, I think you have it all wrong, Lucifer. We take time out for Adoration in order to attune ourselves to the Divine. It allows us to reach a state where we can easily walk the Path of Angels. Somehow we translate that feeling into a special sense of devotion. It is a way of integrating worship into every action in our lives."

"Not worship God? Worship actions? How do you do that?" he asks.

"No, you misunderstand me. I still worship God, it's just that I dedicate my actions to Him. I often utter a prayer with every task I do, blessing my actions for the greater good. This morning, for example. You asked me why I was not at Adoration. It was because I was with several other angels who could not be there."

"Renegades?" he asks. "And what excuse would all of you have for not coming to Adoration?"

"We were with the sick angels, the ones with broken feathers that will not stop molting."

"Why don't they just come to service? Perhaps if God saw them, He would heal them," he says.

"They are too ill to travel," I say. "They cannot walk, let alone fly."

"Why did you not carry them?" he asks.

"Because it is painful for them to travel," I explain.

"Pain in Heaven. Imagine that." He says it in a tone that seems to state the obvious, as if he were explaining things to an ignorant child.

"They wanted to go to Adoration," I say. "Since they could not, I took Adoration to them."

He reacts with feigned surprise. "Took Adoration to them? Which one of you played God Almighty, or did you take turns Adoring each other?"

"It was nothing like that," I say, casting aside his hurtful comments. "We sang, and laid hands upon our sick brethren, and we prayed together with all *our hearts, praising God Almighty who created us and gave us life."*

"Even if it is a sick life?" he asks. He draws a sudden breath and continues questioning: "How did they get sick in the first place? And why does God allow this sickness to persist?"

"They were doing His work in the lands below the Firmament," I reply.

"Ah, yes," he says. "The new frontier. And the illness? How did it come about?"

"We are not sure. They somehow contracted the condition," I say. "We are studying it now, looking for ways to carry on our work in safety. For now, there are limited forays into the Firmament and the lands below. It is dangerous, as we both know."

"Dangerousss," he says. The word leaks out of his mouth, like air escaping a balloon, each syllable hissing from between his lips. "And so you played nursemaid to these unfortunates, consoling them because they could not worship the very Being who sent them to their fates in the first place."

"That was the odd thing," I say. "After a while, they began to feel better. They stopped molting, even if it was temporary. It was as if coming together gave us more strength. You know, Lucifer, there are powers within us, strengths that God has left for us to discover on our own. It is strange that I found them in the service of helping others.

"No," I say. "It's not really strange. In serving others I am serving God. Are we not all God, albeit small pieces of Him. And if that is true, then serving others is indeed the same as serving Him."

"So now God is self serving?" He twists my logic in his usual fashion. "If what you say is true, then in serving me, would you not also be serving God?" He nods in approval. "I like the way you think. Would you mind coming with me and explaining that to some of my followers?"

"Why don't you just stick to steering your ship," I say, trying to draw him away from our conversation. "And leave your followers alone."

He smiles. "You're right." He breathes deep, sighing naturally. "I love steering this ship. I Adore it."

I can't tell if he is being facetious or serious.

"Is that all?" I ask, wary of his quick change of thought. "Or is it just that steering this ship makes you feel like you are in control of something?"

His smile becomes a grin.

Sometimes it is I who make him think.

14. God's Divine Purpose

The scene shifts, now becoming a restaurant kitchen. We are preparing food for a banquet. There is a busy dining room outside the kitchen, filled with the hungry souls of mankind.

I admire the detail at which he can construct and control these scenes. "Why do you create these images? Is this what you imagine to be Mankind's future?" I ask.

"I do not imagine them. They are Mankind's future," he says flatly.

"You know this for fact?" I challenge.

"A fact," he states. "You are seeing part of God's vision for Man. He has shared this vision with me. What do you think?"

"Interesting," I say. I don't know what to think. If this is God's plan, it all looks good to me. Lucifer sees my smile of contentment, of childish interest. These things make him prickly, forcing him back into the

discord that makes him feel more comfortable these days.

"I do not like this new directive from God," he says. He is silent for a moment, judging my reaction. It is his skill, weighing each word and building one idea on top of another until you are drawn into his thoughts.

"What do you mean?" I finally ask.

"At first God creates Angels, telling us our purpose is to serve Him. All right, I agree with that. I love God with all my heart and I can think of nothing I would rather do than serve His divine purpose. But then He creates Man and He gives us a new directive. He puts Man above the Angels. He tells us to serve Man. Don't you think this is odd?"

I think about it for a moment, then say: "Are you jealous of Adam and his kin?"

He spits into a pot of soup in front of him. "How can I be jealous of a lesser creature? What power does Man have that the Angels do not?" He stirs the pot, mixing the ingredients to a Chef's perfection.

"Man has the attention of God, which takes His eye away from you," I say.

This irritates him, I can tell, for I have struck upon a truth. Our conversations often end at this point, or somehow they seem to change towards something different. But I am not the only one he talks to about such things. I soon began to hear his words echoed in other voices, and it disturbed me.

15. Can There Be Discord in Heaven?

"Something puzzles me, Brother," I ask him.

"Speak," he says, his tone regal, as if granting me a privilege.

"You love God above all others," I say.

"All others," he confirms.

"How do you love someone and yet plot against them?"

"If you love someone, there is no plot," he answers. "You have only his or her best interest at heart."

"Yes, but by making choices for someone, even one you love, are you not going against the principles of free will?" I ask.

"I never said I was making choices for God," he replies.

"I am not talking about God, I am talking about love," I say.

"They are one in the same," he says.

"Okay," I say. "But you still haven't answered my question. Can you truly love someone, yet plot against them?"

We are suddenly inside a farmhouse standing in front of a window. Outside the sun is beginning to rise. Some animals move about, casting shadows against the palate of morning colors.

"There are things inside our minds that are kept hidden even from ourselves," he says. "Others can see them, but for some reason that I cannot explain, we can never see them. I believe it has something to do with perspective or point of view. Our eyes face outward and never inward."

I nod silently in agreement. He motions for me to follow him as he walks across the room towards a door that leads to the porch outside. When he opens the door I see that the house is not on safe, level ground, but instead surrounded by a river of lava. The sun that I thought I had seen through the window is a volcano in the distance. The animals that had appeared to be moving gracefully through a meadow are actually cowering from a conflagration that follows close behind them. Ahead of them is a precipice, and the only safe route appears to be towards us, between a narrow path in the lava that is rapidly closing.

"Yes, there is free will," he continues, "And none can interfere with that. I cannot reach my hand out and suddenly change the direction in which those beasts are running. If I call to them, they may not listen, but seeing what fate awaits them, should I not try?"

"And this is what you are trying to do for God? Warn Him of some impending disaster?" I ask.

"Precisely," comes his reply.

"But Lucifer, what if, by pointing out these things, you are changing the destiny of things?"

"If you accept the fact that everything is a part of God's plan, then what difference would it make?" he asks. "Anything I do would be a part of that plan."

"Is not a plan, by the very definition of the word, just that? Only a plan, a guideline for what is intended? Once again, you have taken away free will."

He looks oddly at me, from out of the corner of his eye, and again I see that I have struck something inside of him. He seems to convince himself too easily of these ideas, as if coming to a conclusion first and then building the supporting evidence. This is dangerous. It removes true objectivity.

We spread our wings and lift ourselves off the porch and above the farmhouse. From our new perspective, hovering over the scene, we see that the precipice is not as great as we had thought. The animals are actually herding towards a body of water that lay at the foot of a gently falling slope. It had been hidden from our view, forced upon us by our perspective. Behind the farmhouse more lava burns in molten pools. We watch as the path between the streams of fire that looked safe closes rapidly. Had the animals followed our directions, they would now be trapped.

I do not know whose mind created these images, but the visual representation of the argument is final. The house is quickly engulfed in flames and swallowed up inside the fire.

Lucifer feigns a frown and shakes his head.

"It would seem that the greatest of intentions sometime have the worst results," I say. "Doesn't love demand that you give who or what you love the right to act with free will, in the manner of their own choosing, and not yours? Or, at the very least, discuss things and come to a mutual decision. Are not two perspectives better than one?" I beg to task him on these things, to ask him if he dare to presume what is best for God, but I keep silent.

"You miss the point," he says. Suddenly we find ourselves in a stream of angels flowing gently towards the light, held aloft as if on sunbeams. "But since you touch deeply upon the thoughts that trouble me, perhaps you can help me think things through."

"I love you, Lucifer. You are my brother and my friend," I say. "I am always willing to help with such a task."

"When did this duality of purpose begin?" he asks.

I think about it and I am unable to answer. But like all his questions, Lucifer already knows the answer. His goals are not to seek input from others, but again to stimulate a logical thought process. Someone once named him the Father of All Lawyers. It is a title he well deserves.

"It began when God created the Firmament", he says. "We were all one in the beginning. Then God separated what was above the Firmament from what was below it, and we saw the beginning of duality. Before that time I had but one purpose, to love and serve God. I thought of nothing else. But now, I sense another purpose churning deep inside me."

I sense this unrest within him as well. It is not hidden from view, but I feel his motive is. I want to tell him to give up this folly, but after the demonstration of free will that we have just witnessed, I restrain myself. I do not want to alter the course of things or interfere with the hand of God or my brother.

16. Was It God's Plan, or Lucifer's?

The bubble of memory breaks and we are free. She lays dazed beside me in our celestial hammock. She looks puzzled and confused. "What is it, dear?" I ask.

"I don't understand any of it, Father," she says.

"To tell you the truth, neither do I."

She laughs, and I join her.

"Many of us came to different conclusions about God's motives," I say. "Satan will tell you that the Fallen Angels do God's work, but that is his twisted logic. Even so, by tempting Man, does Lucifer not test humanity for God, as if purifying metals in the hottest fires? Very often Man is at his best in the worst of conditions. I have considered the notion that my brother is in league with God to develop a better quality of human."

She has her own thoughts, though, tending towards compassion. "It's sad that Uncle Lucifer can never come home again."

"Yes, it is," I say. "I think of his loss, of the past we shared before discord tore Heaven apart."

My feelings are transparent to her. "I miss my brother," I say. "I love Lucifer."

"I do too, but I don't know why," she replies. "He looks so different than I expected. He's actually kind of pretty."

"The Hand of God created us both in the same generation of angels. Yet, why do I feel shame for my brother?" Tears cloud my eyes, and she gently places a hand upon my shoulder.

"Yes, Lucifer is my brother," I say to her, "And for that reason more than any other, I drank deeply of his darkened words and considered them carefully. He trusted me with his deepest secrets, even as he pitted me against God and my inmost beliefs. I carried the weight of worry for the course of action he was taking, and in the end he forced upon me a terrible choice, for who could I betray, my Father or my Brother? And if I chose one over the other, how can I avoid betraying myself?"

17. My Choice

We are silent, meditating on what we have talked about and experienced. There is a tug and we are in another memory bubble. Lucifer is talking to me, trying to persuade me to his cause. I remember this memory well, his last attempt to convert me. The oily thickness of the bubble descends upon us and I am drawn into it. My mouth is silent and again we are unable to do anything but observe.

"Join me, my brother," he says, demanding that I pledge to follow him. His power to manipulate matter and create illusion is always present. We are in a courtroom where he stands behind a podium presenting his case.

"How can I go against God?" I ask him, trying to convince him of my convictions. "Would you have us destroy our Father?"

"You overestimate Him," he says. "God is not as all powerful as you think."

"No, you overestimate yourself," I say. He laughs at me, as if I were a naive child. I know it is only his

way of making himself feel superior, but as he looks down on me from a high place I cannot help but feel small and insignificant.

"How can you also go against me, my brother?" he asks. "You know God has abandoned us. He prefers the company of Man to angels. If we are to survive, we must forge ahead and take control of our own destiny."

"I do not believe God has abandoned us," I tell him. "In fact, he has made us a part of His new plan."

"To serve Man?" he retorts. "Again, I think you overestimate God."

"Lucifer, how can I convince you that you are brewing trouble? Abandon these thoughts and let God's love cleanse you of these misdeeds."

"There are no misdeeds. If you see a mistake, do you lay silent, or do you correct it? God has made a mistake."

He comes from behind the podium and approaches me. "Listen," he says, grabbing me by the shoulders and forcing me to face him. "We can realign Heaven's purpose and the role of Man in the

Universe. I know God's weakness, and I have assembled an army of angels to support my cause. I have only to mark the time for the revolt and it will happen. I want you to join me. If you do I will reward you for your allegiance with a place of honor by my side."

He lets those words hang in the air before us, waiting for me to swear an oath to him. "And if I don't?" I ask.

He looks away. The podium turns black, becoming a funeral pyre. I wonder whose body lay draped beneath the shroud. "I cannot be responsible for the behaviors of my army," he says. "Free will, you know."

"Are you saying you won't protect me?" I ask.

"I am neither saying nor guaranteeing anything," he says. "This just cause that I support demands loyalty, and there are those who believe you are either with us or against us."

"You know I will not take up arms against our Father," I say. "Or you, for that matter."

"I'm not asking you to fight. I'm asking you to lead. You're clever, like me. We work well together. Think of the successes of all our missions together. This is just one more adventure."

"That ends in our Father's... What? Death?"

18.   A Confused Tyrant

"God is a confused tyrant," he says. "At first He tells us to bow to no one but Him, then He tells us to bow to Man. Why this contradiction? He offers angels no other position in His kingdom but to serve Man. Do you want that? Do you not yearn only to serve God? And what do we really know about this new creation anyway?"

He pauses, waiting for me to digest that thought.

"Man is not worthy of elevation above the angels, despite what God has decreed," he says. "This new divine creation is flawed, and given time this will bear out to be true. I have tried to convince God of this, but He will hear nothing of it."

"What argument did you present to Him?" I ask, curious about what he could possibly tell the Creator that He did not already know, especially about His own creation.

The world about us shifts, becoming an artist's shop, a potter's wheel spinning on a nearby bench. Lucifer is playing with our surroundings again. "Man thinks he is in Paradise. Eden, it is called." He sits behind the wheel and begins to work the clay, slamming it with his hands and beating it into shape. "But it is not so. Man was fashioned out of clay, the coarse matter that lies below the Firmament. And then he is given dominion over all the beasts and plants of the field. Are you telling me that this Man is more powerful than a lion? Or a jackal?"

"I don't know," I say. "I have not seen Man. What does he look like?"

"He was created in God's image," says Lucifer, pulling the clay into a miniature homunculus.

"As are we," I remind him. "And if Man is indeed created in God's image, then does he not have God's wisdom and His talent to create?"

He laughs. "You assume too much, my brother. What was once clay at my feet will always be so." He presses his fingers into the clay he was molding and it again becomes a shapeless mass. "Do you know that all God demands of Man is that he not partake of the fruit of the Tree of Life?"

"The Tree of Life?" I ask. "I don't know about it. What fruit does this tree bear?"

"It is also called the Tree of Knowledge of Good and Evil," he says. "By eating the fruit, so it is said, you will gain all God's knowledge and power."

There is a strange look in his eye. "Do you covet this fruit yourself?" I ask, curious about the power this crop holds over him.

He smiles, answering my question with a nod.

"Then I fear for you," I say. "Desire can lead to intense yearning and suffering."

"I know," he says.

"Do you want the responsibility that comes with that knowledge? God's power is not something to wish for lightly," I say.

The artist's shop dissolves around us and we are now in a garden filled with fruit trees. "Why would God not want Man to have this knowledge? Why taunt Man by telling him that there even exists such a thing as this fruit?" he asks.

"To keep him happy, of course," I say. "A child should not bear the burdens of an adult, so why force these things upon them. Besides, there is a time for maturity, and perhaps God knows that this fruit will harm Man if taken prematurely. Surely you would protect any child from his own ignorance. Will not God reveal to Man everything in His own time?"

"Perhaps," he says. "I don't know, but I plan to try this fruit myself."

"Oh, don't act so surprised," he says, reading my reaction. "There is no taboo against me trying the fruit. God has only forbidden Man to eat of it, not the Angels."

"What do you hope to gain by this?" I ask him.

"Knowledge, of course," he says. "If I am to rule in God's place, then I need His wisdom."

"And what of Man after you wrest control of Heaven from God?" I ask.

"Man can have his Eden for all I care. He is so stupid that he does not realize that he is in a prison. The Garden has a wall around it, restricting his freedom. What kind of paradise restricts freedom?"

"Perhaps the wall is for Man's protection," I suggest.

"From the beasts he has dominion over?" he asks cynically. "No, God keeps His new creation distracted. He has even named his pet. He calls it Adam. He recently created a companion for Adam in case His pet gets bored. He calls the companion Eve. All he asks is they be happy and live in the garden together. They have no sense of purpose other than this."

"They are children," I say. "New to the world. What would you expect of them?"

"Mark me, they will disappoint God one day," he vows.

"And you will not?" I ask.

He glares at me and we are back at the funeral pyre. Suddenly it ignites in flames. I stand back while the fire radiates heat and smoke, curling up into a clear sky that quickly becomes shadowed with black clouds.

"No, you disappoint me, brother," he says. "I offer you a position at my side and you refuse. So be it. I refuse you as well. You are in a minority of angels who remain myopic, blinded by your closeness to God. We will see who is the mightier, God or I. I shall have my kingdom, and you shall have your reward, whatever that may be. With Heaven gone, you will be outcast and wander the wastelands. Ultimately you have no choice but to join me, you just don't see it yet. I only hope you live long enough to make the right choice."

"You are a fool, Lucifer," I say defiantly. "Don't you know we are all immortal?"

He sneers. "I will tell you if that is true, or whether it is another lie told to you by God to keep you in fear of Him. I will tell you the truth after I have tasted the Fruit of the Tree of Knowledge."

19. To Thy End I Dedicate This Throne

Fast forward, we move again, bubbles whooshing by like wind across our minds. After that last conversation, Lucifer went to the Garden and found the forbidden tree. He wasted no time in helping himself to a generous portion of the fruit. It had no real effect on him, for he already possessed the knowledge that it promised. The fruit itself contained no magic elixir, nor any secret power or knowledge. Later I realized it was not the fruit, but the forbidden act that imparted the knowledge of good and evil. By disobeying God and eating the fruit, Man's innocence was lost, and thus his fall from Grace began. Lucifer must have realized that it was his actions that caused the change in him and not the fruit. I could see it the next time we met.

"Come, my brother," he says. "Let me show you something." The air around us swirls, and at first I suspect it is another shifting illusion of his, but then I grasp the solidity of this new setting. It is a real place.

We are alone in a long hall in a temple atop a high mountain. Far below us lay the Plains of Heaven, the fertile fields of God's kingdom. At one end of the hall sits a tall, ornate chair on a raised dais. He escorts me up the steps where I watch him seat himself with the flourish of an emperor. When I turn around, I see that we are no longer alone. The hall is filled with angels bent to his word. They genuflect, tapping their hearts as they swear allegiance to Lucifer. "Where did they come from?" I ask.

"They feel my presence and are called to me whenever I sit upon my throne. Look, my brother, for this is where I will rule my kingdom."

"You dare put yourself above God," I say, seeing the obvious symbolism in this throne. "How arrogant!" I exclaim. "You have no idea…"

He waves his hand and, seeing the look in his follower's eyes, I silence myself. He is not offended by my words, but in him I see a new confidence that was not there before. "It is you who have no idea," he says. "You forget what I have consumed. I know things you cannot possibly know, things that are not even in your vocabulary." He stands and pushes me down the steps, a performance for his attending audience.

"The knowledge I have gained has made me invincible," he says, his voice becoming louder as he fills the hall with his words. "And I know God's *weakness! With my throne established, the time to confront God has arrived." He calls his armies close to him. More arrive, filling the empty spaces in the far reaches of the hall. I hear the crowd banter as they begin to plot the first of many campaigns against the Holy of Holies.*

I want to stay and listen, but instead I slip away as his men gather around him. He basks in their affection and admiration, reveling that it was he who had the courage to eat the forbidden fruit. They trust his newfound knowledge, believing in the power he has gained. I am surprised at how freely they give their allegiance.

There is a pang of fear growing in my heart. I do not know where to turn. I need God's guidance, but I feel unworthy of His council. I have witnessed my brother's treachery, and I am as guilty as he. My crime is inaction. I placate myself by believing that any course I take against Lucifer would be ineffective. If I can not stop him with words, how can I hope to stop him with violence?

But in the presence of Almighty God, the Father, He will see through me and know the truth. A loyal son would have gone to Him long before now. I sit alone outside my brother's palace, pounding my head, hoping something will change inside.

I am forsaken.

20. A Stone in My Heart

The experience fades and my daughter and I are propelled to another part of my mind, another bubble of time long gone. Again I am cast as an uneasy participant in the events of my past, the price I pay for this reenactment. I long to speak and change the dark history about to unfold before us, but I am powerless. The thoughts of that day swirl around me like the flotsam of so many wasted hours. They congeal, clinging to me like tropical humidity, a dampness that permeates my core.

Adoration does not help me. Secrets lay hidden in my heart, and now I find it difficult to open myself to God's grace. Have I been infected with the same disease that Lucifer suffers from? How long before I defect to my brother's side? I begin to notice that I am not the only one afflicted. I can see things in my fellow angels that I have not seen before: unrest, secrets behind eyes of fire, faint murmurings, and dark spots that cast shadows upon their golden cloaks.

With so much tension building, something must give. Even as my brother warns me, I am not prepared for the first skirmish.

It happens during Adoration and Worship. Heavy with secret sin, I hide in the throng and pray for forgiveness. I invite God's grace into my heart, but it flows around the dark stone inside me and settles like a river of oil around my heart.

God draws our attention, choosing this time to reveal a vision of His divine plan. He shows us Man and Woman, introducing His creation formally to us. Once again He bides us to bow before this new creation, serving Man as we would God. I look at this puny thing, this animated clay figurine, and I see what Lucifer tried to tell me. These creatures do not possess the brightness of angels, nor even wings with which to fly. They appear tainted, created from some part below the Firmament, stained with dirt and coarse matter.

But I hear God's command. Some angels bend quickly to His will, and as I begin to lower my eyes and my head, I notice some are not assuming a posture of subservience. I see Lucifer, his head bobbing as he makes his way through the crowd. He looks at me and smiles knowingly. His eyes dart toward God with evil intent then flash back to mine as we lock gazes. I am frozen, my body bent forward as I am about to bow down. He shakes his head slowly from side to side, as if disappointed, even disgusted, with me.

He becomes animated. "You don't have to bow down," he shouts to everyone, but I know the words are meant for me. His eyes direct them so. Everyone turns towards him. He holds their attention and continues speaking. "I, for one, will not bow down to Man, and neither should you." There is anger in his voice.

The voice of God answers, filled with an equal amount of love. "Why do you disobey me, Lucifer?" He asks.

"I don't disobey you, My Lord," he says humbly. "I simply do not understand. You once said that we should bow to no being but you, and now you decree otherwise."

"Yes, beloved one, I did say that. Now I wish you to bow to Man. I want you to help him, for he is fragile in My ways and I need you to help teach him and guide him."

"But why, O Lord? Are we not good enough?" asks Lucifer. "Why this change? If Man knows not your ways, then why elevate him above all angels?"

With every iota of love, God answers, "Because it is My will, and you are all My children, both Man and Angel. Neither is elevated more than the other."

Lucifer begins to cry. He is moved by so much love. I feel it too, we all do. Even Man and Woman, present in their dream bodies, close in the company of God, feel overwhelming divine love. It is the Almighty trying to heal us all.

My brother hunches over, his face cast down. I can see him struggling with powerful thoughts. He shakes his head, talking to himself, muttering random words and partial phrases. I sense that his twisted logic has turned inward. He refuses God's love and allows his tears to turn to anger. The love drains from his body and his skin begins to redden.

I move closer to him, my goal to lay a hand on his shoulder so that he may know comfort. I reach out and he turns away, brushing against my forearm as he deflects my advance. His wing slaps me in the face as he pushes me away.

Lucifer does not tarry. From beneath his cloak he draws a blade, a special knife. I do not its history or how he acquired it, but I can see that it holds some special power and significance. It moves in his hand, a jewel encrusted dagger with dark markings on the blade. Light glistens and reflects off it as it twists in his hand. With a practiced move he coils, his hand arcs over his shoulder. With all his might I see him flick the knife toward God.

21.   Divine Blood

I, like many of us, am frozen into inaction by Satan's bold move. Violence against the Creator! In the history of Heaven, it had never been imagined. I stand in fear as the dagger travels its deadly path.

Not all are frozen. Tarshish, an Angel of the inmost Host, thrusts himself between God and the advancing blade. It strikes him high in the chest with an abrupt choonk sound. His arm ignites in a beacon of flames and light, spreading through his body until he turns transparent. I see the blade suspended inside his body, clear and lucid, as if trapped beneath a wall of ice. His face furrows with pain. His body becomes a statue as he falls from the sky to land at God's feet, lying still and silent as he slowly fades from existence.

The followers of Lucifer are spread thin through the choir of angels. They erupt with unexpected violence. Some draw staffs and knives from beneath their cloaks and plunge them into unsuspecting angels beside them. Others use hooks, tossing them with expert guidance where they gouge into the wings of helpless angels.

Wounded and denied of flight, the hooks tear bigger holes as their victims struggle to break free.

Michael wastes no time. From under his cloak I see him draw The Sword, aware of his duty to protect Man. He motions for loyal angels from his legion to join him. They form a shield of protection around Adam and Eve to guard them as they escort them away to safety.

There is carnage everywhere. A nearby angel lies bleeding from the wings. One wing hangs limp while a dark stain leaks from his side. Another is blind, clasping her hands over bloodied eye sockets as she cries for help. Another is missing the lower part of his body. He flaps his wings and flails his arms, slapping the ground like a fresh caught fish. I see lines drawn as friend and foe become known to each other. A wall of protectors forms between the blind angel and Lucifer's men. Armed with swords and spears, they poke and jab at each other. One of the protectors is blessed with incredible speed. He dodges lethal blows from swords. Then his image blurs and he suddenly appears behind Lucifer's men where he strikes them unconscious.

The ever present sound of the Heavenly Choir has stopped, replaced by the deafening clang of metal. I duck down low just as one of Lucifer's minions takes a swipe at me with a rapier. A comrade sees I am in trouble. Nirgal hits my attacker on the head with a heavy golden cup. He strikes with such force that it knocks the cup from his hand.

There are angels everywhere fighting each other, the peace of Heaven gone in an eruption of fury. Madness, brother fighting brother, as if we are not in Heaven any more, instead conveyed to some morbid battlefield far from the circle of God's Light. I want it to disappear like some background illusion, a shifting reflection of my brother's psyche, but it will not go away. This is real.

Nirgal nods to me and moves on, drawn into the conflict as he tries to save another. The prone figure of my adversary lies unconscious on the ground before me, both the cup and the sword lying beside him. As if it were a choice, I wonder if I should take up the sword as my brother has, or should I hold the cup of goodness in my hands?

Lucifer's band has the upper hand, but then Michael returns. "Man is safe," he reports to God. "Guarded by the Cherubim." He salutes God with his Sword and holds it forward in respect. The Creator touches the tip and nods at the Archangel. Michael understands. He lifts himself and flies over the crowd, swiping again and again as he guides the Sword of Fire with terrible purpose. Angels lose limbs. Weapons melt and burn when touched by The Sword. He points it at his enemies and fire spits forth to burn holes in their skin. Friend and foe *seem identical and I wonder how he tells them apart, or are there innocents that also suffer because of this violence?*

The tide appears to turn, and Lucifer draws back for a moment, rallying his men. He makes a series of cryptic gestures and they assume new positions. Michael charges at a wall they have formed, but instead of resisting him they merely separate, allowing him to fly uncontested between them. Before Michael can change direction they close in on him, keeping him occupied as the rest of them spread into a pattern.

"Look what is happening!" I shout. "They are opening a path between Lucifer and God." It is a protected gauntlet, the walls face outward to discourage attackers.

Lucifer picks up a pike, a long stick sharpened at one end. He kisses the tip. With all his might he drives it forward, a mighty cry bellows from his lungs as he lunges, following the path to his Creator. Defending angels step aside in fear at his advance, unaware that they help him.

I scream, but it is too late. The pike finds a weak spot in God's left side. It tears the robe and pierces the skin, driving inward until it stops and hangs half out of His body like a broken tree branch. A dark stain mars the Supreme Being's robes.

God writhes. Is it from the pain of Lucifer's betrayal or the wound now gaping in His side?

There is silence on the battlefield, so quiet we hear random, whispered comments.

"God can bleed."

"Is there no immortality?"

"Can this be the end of our Father's Heaven?"

"Oh, my faith!"

God's voice breaks the relative silence, clear and strident it carries across the plain. "Lucifer," He says with all sadness. The battle stops as all eyes turn toward God. He slowly pulls the spear out and examines it carefully before thrusting it aside.

God's eyes show love and sadness all at once. He too seems astonished. "How could you?" He asks. "My favorite." He touches His side where it bleeds. The blood stains his finger and drips dark and sticky off it. "I love you, Lucifer. More than you will ever know."

It that moment my brother realizes the extent of his sin. His hands fall to his sides. His followers look to him for orders.

I act automatically, seeing the stain of blood stretch from God's side. I pick up the fallen cup and run forward, maneuvering to catch the dripping blood. I tear His robe and press my hand to the side of God as if I could stay the flow. It seeps around it and blood slowly begins to fill the cup.

As if unaware of my motion, God continues to address Lucifer. "Why do you betray me?" He asks. "What do you hope to gain?"

"A kingdom," answers Lucifer.

"Then you shall have it," replies the Creator.

I look in the cup and the blood turns dark. A moist stain hides the golden metal that contains it. The Light of Heaven grows dim and grey clouds circle above us.

God speaks again, His eyes glowing. "Heaven cannot hold two rulers, my son," He says. Rain begins to fall. It has never rained in Heaven and it pelts us now like rocks, damping our cloaks and wetting our wings. Wind begins to blow and God raises His voice above it. "Therefore you must go!"

22. Hell? No!

God speaks with finality. The hostility starts anew and Heaven shakes, a quake of such magnitude that we all are caught off balance. The fighting ends quickly as Lucifer and his men retreat, disappearing in the grey rain that begins to fall everywhere. Some of the loyal angels take pursuit, but most huddle protectively around God.

I step away, still holding the chalice of blood in my hands. I no longer feel safe, but neither do those around me. It is a tense moment as some of Lucifer's followers remain in the crowd waiting to observe what will happen now. I walk away from the Creator through the pressing crowd that surrounds me. The air is filled with recriminations and interrogations as the loyal and the disloyal try to cull each other out.

The rain continues to pelt us, the ground to shake with sudden uncertainty. "This is insane," I utter. I stare at the cup as Heaven's rain begins to wash the stain.

An angel is beside me. She covers the top of the chalice with her hand. "God's blood is power," she whispers. "You must keep this safe."

Another angel is at my side echoing her concern. "Yes. You need to take this sacred relic from the field of battle."

"Even temporary sanctuary would be desirable to this."

I agree. As we turn to leave there is a wounded angel on the ground. My escort steps over him and the angel lets out a cry.

"Are you all right?" I ask, bending to his side.

He opens his cloak revealing a hole near his heart. Blood pumps and ebbs from the wound and he agonizes with each pulse. His hands clasp his chest. "It lies open," he says, his voice difficult and hoarse. "Lucifer has inflicted a grave wound on my heart."

He is attended by one who is known to me, Paraqlitos. "God is not the only one who lost blood today," says the angel of sorrow and death.

It is a mystical wound, tearing itself apart and rebuilding itself with every beat. He is in constant pain. I look in the chalice and see the blood fresh in the bottom. I hover over him, allowing a drop to spill into his wound.

The rain falls, turning the drop of blood into a dark rivulet that flows into the hole. The agony on his face remains and there is no miraculous cure. The wound on his chest opens and closes with regularity.

I place my hand on his chest for comfort. "It appears that I have failed you," I say. With all my heart I wish him well, uttering silent prayers to God.

He hears me praying, and in between raspy breaths he speaks. "God bless us," he says, turning to Paraqlitos. "Go, my friend. There are more important needs to attend to than my own."

A cry comes from the mob surrounding God. "The wound is healed!" Gasps and sighs roll through the crowd like thunder. A base line of chatter builds, filled with hopefulness. I yearn for the heavenly choir, but there is only this underscore of prattle.

"God is whole again."

"A miracle!"

"Praise God."

"Amen and Halleluiah."

We hear these and other comments but also the murmured renunciations of Lucifer's minions. They begin to leave the crowd, moving toward the fringes of the mob. One passes near us and looks down at our misery with a sneer and a chuckle.

My raspy breathed friend answers the sneer from the pit of his suffering. "See? I am alive," he says. "God is stronger than Lucifer."

Paraqlitos draws our attention down. "Look. He is healing. With every heartbeat the hole lessens."

The evidence is plain. We watch the wound knit itself well. His side heals and even the stain fades from his cloak.

Our antagonist stops, astonishment replacing his sneer. He turns toward God with reverence and his face glows with the Light of Goodness. He smiles as he raises his hands toward his heart in blessing. But as he looks down, they are dirty and stained with blood. His hands hold a knife. He stares at it, childlike and sad, twisting the blade as his thoughts consume him. His face saddens as the Light fades and he turns to walk away from us.

Before he takes a step an angel is at his side. He puts an arm gently around him, straightens his posture, and slowly turns him back toward the Light. "God forgives," he says. "As do I."

He looks at us and we nod in agreement. He smiles back. They turn and walk with venerable steps toward the crowd, moving closer to God. The knife slips from his hand and falls, dropping through a hole that opens through Heaven's floor.

The grey rain continues to fall, hiding the retreat of those who escape to fight another day. The remainder of Lucifer's men are uneasy, too tired or too beaten to retreat. Members of the Malake Habbalah, the Angels of Punishment, gather them up, unsure of what to do with them except keep them contained.

It is a strange sensation. The Heavenly Choir is silent, replaced by the rain and thunder and the strange grinding sound whenever the foundation of Heaven shakes beneath our feet. As odd as they sound these are preferable to the noise of battle.

It is soothing.

"The rain washes us clean," says Paraqlitos.

"God's blood is power," I say. I have been shielding the cup from the rain with my arm. There is a golden plate lying on the ground nearby. I take it and cover the chalice, then tear a piece of my robe off and wrap it in the cloth. I carefully hold it upright lest I spill the last of its precious contents. I open my cloak and tuck it in excess garment, securing it upright to my waist.

The rain does not feel threatening now. Instead it washes the stains and the sins from us. I feel renewed.

23. God's New Decree

"Michael," calls God. "You must drive this refuse from Heaven. Cast them out of the gates and into the pit that lies beyond the Firmament."

My brethren cry out like a mob. How unlike angels, to behave like this. Nevertheless, Malake Habbalah surge around the Fallen Ones and gather them up in a chaotic mass.

"To the gates," I hear a cry.

Joined by another. "Cast them out."

"Banishment!" And on and on.

We move along, a surging sea of souls. The conversations around me reveal much. Some of my brethren are calling for more blood, others demand love and understanding. We are divided, each of us struggling to come to grips with these sudden events in Heaven. I follow along, caught up in the frenzy and the desire to see what will happen next.

Mbriel hastens to me, eager to speak. "Ho, my friend," he says. "How do I find you this day?"

"Please," I say. "Your brevity is misplaced. Do you believe this chaos?"

"I take no part in it," he says.

"You side with none?" I ask.

"I am not the only one," he says. "I am an angel of the wind, and why should I fight? There are plenty willing to do so in my place."

Swords clang in the distance. A cry goes out. "Slay them." A Malake Habbalah jabs a captive who roars with indifference. Lucifer's men put up little fight. Their numbers are few and they do not resist the fate that awaits them

"These are the defeated," I say. "The dangerous ones are somewhere within the gates still plotting the overthrow of Heaven."

"If we only knew where they were hiding."

I think of my brother's palace and wonder if he occupies his throne. My thoughts churn anew. My hand clutches the chalice beneath my robes. Too many choices. "Why not stay neutral," I say aloud.

Mbriel nods.

No quarter or mercy is allotted to Lucifer's men. Heavy hands push them outside the protective aura of Heaven. Their wounds begin to heal, a miracle that soon becomes a nightmare. Limbs grow back scabbous and misshapen. Some of their wings turn from light and feathery to pointed and hairy, webbed with fleshy leather. Each fallen comrade seems to take on a shape that reflects the hideousness of their heart. One sees horns appear on his head in place of a crown he once wore. Still another, freshly limbless from battle with the flaming Sword, finds his remaining arms and legs sealed into waxy stubs. Another watches his hands turn to hooves as he falls to all fours and cries like a beast. I know him as Raym, once of the order of thrones, consigned now as a creature of a different order.

Denied the Grace of God, this parade of Fallen Angels presses onward, the heat of Michael's Sword close behind them. There, flung wide before the gates of Heaven, Michael drives them out, aided by Gadiel, Kazviel, Heikhali, and other Gate Angels of various orders. Beaten and wounded they fall from the precipice outside the gate. Some cannot fly, while others drop like wounded birds that flap in desperation. Some cry for mercy only to feel the tip of the flaming Sword.

"A pitiful band indeed," says Mbriel.

24. Guard Duty

"We have done God's bidding," says Michael. His voice carries across the mob and we listen. "I will return and report the success of our deeds. We must seek His council and guidance in these times of discord. Guard well the gates of Heaven from all directions, for there remains an enemy yet inside these walls."

"Lucifer!" shouts an angry angel.

"Find him!" cries another.

"If we cast him out he will return," shouts a third. "We must destroy him."

There are frantic suggestions on what course to follow. Mbriel whispers to me. "This is not good."

Michael flaps his wings and rises above us. He swings The Sword over his head in an artful display of skill. It hums with power, drawing everybody's attention. The crowd grows silent and he settles to speak again. "We are the Loyal. We carry out God's will as He decrees. Let there be no more talk. Only God sits in judgment, and it is His justice we should seek."

"God is great," shouts an angel.

"Amen," comes a chorus.

"Katzfiel, you are in charge here until I return," says Michael.

"Ahhh," whispers Mbriel. "The Sword of Lightning replaces the Sword of Fire. Nice choice. If anyone can keep order here it is Katzfiel."

"I agree," I say. "This could easily get out of hand."

The crowd parts and Michael passes back through the Gates of Heaven. A few angels follow while the rest take up positions of watchful alert. Many are armed with weapons, both forged and improvised. Katzfiel nods his approval as he inspects the troops.

I stand close inside the gate. Michael glances sideways at me as he walks by. He can see in my heart that I do not side with my brother, but he has that look, as if I have betrayed both him and God. I want to rush forward and stop him, tell him that he can find them hiding in the mountains. My lips seem to betray me, mouthing what I can not utter.

"Upon a high peak there lies a false temple where Lucifer mounts his throne. Go there and find him. Let he and his followers be cast from Heaven."

I think the words but I do not say them. Michael looks away and continues on before I can stop him. The Sword of Fire is safely scabbard at his side, its power at rest.

My thoughts are of Lucifer and I cry for his soul. I wonder if the blood of God can wash away his sins. I would gladly use the cup for my brother's salvation, but I must be sure. Should I bring it to him? Will he welcome me, or even welcome the thought of salvation, let alone the opportunity? Or will God's blood destroy him, a mere drop on his skin enough to melt him away?

I want to run to him with these things, discuss them as we always have. My brother is clever. He can find a way out of this.

I strike the thought from my mind as quickly as it arises, surprised to find myself again drawn into an inner debate over whom to choose, God or my brother.

"Something wrong, friend?" asks Mbriel.

There are shouts from outside the gates, the sound reaching us deftly as most of it is absorbed by the void that surrounds Heaven. We listen to the guards chatter. There is fear and anxiety in their voices.

"False reports," says Mbriel. "We'll be imagining the Fallen Ones in the shadows forever, thinking they plot their return at every opportunity."

"Are you afraid?" I ask. I assess myself, turning the question inward as well.

Mbriel sighs. "No. Not really. But we are under the protection of Heaven. The guards outside the gates certainly feel different."

"By that logic, wouldn't Lucifer's followers also be protected?"

"Hmmm… Interesting thought," he says. "I wonder where they are now," he says.

I look away, stung by the knowledge I have.

Mbriel's eyes narrow as he stares into my soul. He suspects something, but quickly hides his reaction. "I mean the outcasts. Do you think they were injured when thrown over the precipice?"

"Injury?" I respond. "What about the twisted bodies and mutated shapes they became?"

"What about that?" says Mbriel. "Are they outward reflections of their twisted hearts and misplaced loyalties? Is it the vengeance of an angry God?"

"I don't know," I say. I wonder what twisted shape my brother would assume outside the protection of Heaven. It was he who perpetrated this vile event, the reason for the disharmony in Heaven.

25. How Dost Thou Side?

My thoughts are interrupted. The crowd at the gate has swollen to three times its former size. It is a restless mob, filled with speculation and concerns. The conversation reflects what we all feel in our hearts and minds.

"They won't return," I hear one say. "They will cower until Lucifer has joined them. He is their leader. Without him they are a body without a head."

"They're too wounded to try anything," says another. "Did you see how misshapen they've become?"

"I wouldn't want to lose God's Grace," I hear another say.

"Serves them right," interjects someone else.

"I don't know," says a soft voice behind me. "I think there must be a better way out of this than destroying or banishing those we love. I know many

of those angels. We all know them. They are our friends."

"Look at us," comes another gentle voice. "We have armed ourselves and we are prepared to do violence. Does this not go against all we have gained through Love?"

"Is it right to justify violence in the name of good?" questions another.

A loud voice warms us all. "The evil ones will destroy God along with the rest of us if we do not defend ourselves."

Mbriel speaks to me in a whisper amidst all this. "More questions than answers," he says. "And look at the crowd. How many angels are here?"

An angel next to Mbriel overhears us and speaks. "Yes. And how many are out searching? How many protecting God?"

"And how many on the other side," says Zoniel, one I recognize. "Lucifer's numbers may be greater than we estimate."

"How many indeed?" I remark. I try to remember how many I saw in his Kingdom Hall in the mountains. Perhaps a third of us.

"They are among us even now." Zoniel scans the crowd, searching the faces for signs of allegiance or dishonor. "And where do your loyalties lie?" she asks, her eyes fixed on my face.

I am silent, unwilling to share my connection to Lucifer and my knowledge of his plans. Zoniel shakes her head. She turns and weaves into the crowd, reading faces and burning them into the book of good and evil she is writing in her mind.

She is out of range. I whisper my answer. "I have no allegiance."

My words are not unheard. "Don't say that," says Mbriel. "Surely you side with God."

I touch the cup at my belt for reassurance. True, I have not sided with the righteous, but neither am I bound to the devil that my brother has become. "There must be a Middle Way," I say. "I tire from the pain of indecision. There must be a way to reconcile the horrors of my choice. Or lack of choice."

"What choice?" asks Mbriel.

Again our words are overheard. "There is always a choice, and with it duality," says one known to me as Nilaihah. "Every deed we do has both good and evil consequences. The best we can do is hope for good in our actions, tending towards that end. That is why it is so important to think about consequences before taking action."

"Yes," I say. "How can we claim we are doing good when we are so ready to destroy those we once loved?"

"Ones we still love," says Mbriel.

"Heaven has changed," I say. "It is as if we have all tasted the Forbidden Fruit."

26. A Bold Plan

"What is that you keep clutching at your belt?" asks Mbriel.

"What?" I say. My words try to hide what I cannot.

"Open your cloak there," says Nilaihah. "Is that a weapon you have?"

"No," I say flatly. "No weapon. Only a cup." I press the wrapper of cloth close around the chalice revealing its shape. I can feel it. It weighs heavy in my hand with responsibility.

"May I see that?" asks Nilaihah.

"It's only a cup," I say. I change the subject. "Do you know what lies beyond the gates?" I ask.

"Outside Heaven?" asks Nilaihah. "I have been there."

"So have I," says an angel beside him.

"This is Vassago," says Nilaihah, identifying him for me. "He's been beyond the Firmament and back."

"Need a guide?" asks Vassago.

"I've been there a few times," I say. With my brother, my mind adds.

"Why this curiosity?" asks Mbriel.

"If you wanted to conceal something, something not safe to leave in Heaven, where would you take it?"

"There are many places," says Rochel, a friend of Nilaihah and Vassago. "What is the object?"

"This cup," I say.

27. The Truth

"I know little of the realms beyond Heaven. I have not seen the Garden of Eden or much of the Earth, but I have heard other angels speak about them. I know roughly where things might lie, but need more. Would any of you be able to provide me with a map?"

"A map?"

"Of what lies beyond Heaven?"

"Are you planning a trip?" asks Mbriel. "Without me?"

"You can't go out there," says Vassago. "Not now."

"I do not fear the Fallen Ones," I say.

"Maybe you should," says a nearby voice. "Especially out there. Did you see the horrific shapes they assumed? They would tear an angel like you apart in seconds with their claws."

"Which is why you can't go," says Mbriel. "If you leave the aura of Heaven, you'll turn into a monster too."

"That's nonsense," I say.

"It's not," he says, lowering his voice to a whisper that only I can hear. "I did not hear you pledge your allegiance to God. You will change once you pass through the gates."

"No," I say.

"How can you be so sure?" he asks.

"I'll prove it," I say.

"You're not considering what I think you are," he says.

I give him a final look of determination and walk away. The crowd parts easily and I hear the same conversations being replayed around me. As I work my way towards the gates, I realize Mbriel is close behind.

"Where are you going?" asks Zerachiel, a guard at the gate.

"I'm leaving," I say.

Another guard, Pachdiel, approaches. "No one enters or leaves without Michael's permission," he says.

"What about the angels over there?" I ask, indicating a group huddled outside the gate.

"I don't know about them," he says. "My business is this gate."

"I'm going to talk to them," I say.

"No you're not," he says. He raises his weapon and I see his fellow guards posture behind him. "You can wait over there for Michael to return. Now, get!"

There is an altercation nearby. "He's one of them," I hear someone shout. Fighting erupts, first between two angels, growing quickly to include more. The guards react and all attention turns away from us.

I look toward the group outside the gates. They appear normal. I move slowly and cautiously towards the boundary of the Kingdom.

"Don't do it," says Mbriel. He hangs back.

I inch past the guards while they are distracted. The fight grows larger and out of control. Swords clang between shouts and cries. Guards surround two angels who are being driven towards the gates with vehemence. Spears and swords swipe and jab at them. At the gates they are pushed outside.

The crowd watches in awe at what happens next.

The first angel screams as his skin turns blood red. He rushes back towards the gate seeking a return only to be met with spears, pikes, and a line of resistance. Jabbed by weapons he curses them and turns, his head reforming into a grotesque shape that barely resembles his former self. He drops down on all fours, braying like an animal as he spits fire at the lines of defense.

From the darkness beyond the precipice there is a kindred cry. The transformed angel stops and listens, growls one more time, then plunges over the precipice.

The second angel lies dirty on the ground. Nothing has happened to her. She stands defiant before the guards. "See? Nothing," she shouts, turning around for all to see. "I told you I was loyal."

"No you're not," says Pachdiel. "I heard you proclaim that you have no allegiances. Heaven is for the loyal."

"Heaven is for everyone," she says. There is laughter and they turn their backs to her.

She rushes the gate to get back in. Weapons are drawn. A spear point pierces her arm and she backs away. Her hand covers the wound staying the flow of blood.

I instinctively rush to her side. "Show mercy," I shout at the guards. "Can't you see she is friendly?" I realize that I am outside the gates now. My skin tingles, but no magical transformation.

"He's one of them," shouts Mbriel, pointing a finger at me. "I heard him say the same thing just a moment ago. He will not fight with the Lord."

"I know him," shouts another. "He's Lucifer's confidante."

"Yes! Yes!" adds another voice. The frenzy grows.

I look back in astonishment. Mbriel points a finger, Nilaihah beside him, a fist full of hatred shaking in the air. Pachdiel and Zerachiel plant thier feet firmly, their weapons in readiness.

The wounded angel looks at me. "Come on," she says. "We're not welcome here."

28. Holly

We leave the light of the gates but not before I get a good look at my fellow outcast. She has golden hair tainted with flecks of autumn red. An iridescent halo floats gently above her head. Her eyes of azure sparkle like the sea on a moonlight night. Robes of golden white conceal a strong but delicate frame. She fluffs her wings and extends them, shaking something free of them. They are strong and twice the size I expect, larger than her whole body.

I look away and slowly move towards the precipice, peering over the edge to see if there is any sign of the Fallen Ones. I see only rock which forms a steep cliff, ending in mists and clouds that obscure anything that might lie below. There is a cry from the depths, then two in unison. The Fallen One has found his brethren.

I look around. There is a group of angels huddled nearby, the same ones I observed earlier. "I wonder if they are outcasts like us," I ask.

"Yes, we are," says a voice beside me. One of the group has approached us. "I'm sorry. I am Cael. What is it you have there?" he asks.

"I wonder if it is safe." The cup vibrates at my side and I have my answer. I slowly free it from my belt. When I remove the cloth that covers it, the cup comes alive with light, glowing from within. I remove the plate on top and a bright, blinding light radiates upward and out of the cup. We turn away, our eyes unable to look at it.

I am surprised. "When did it transform from a dark spot of blood into this new form?" I say.

"What is it?" asks the wounded angel.

"It is the blood of God, spilled by the spear thrown by Lucifer," I say.

"So, you're the one," she says. "The Grail Angel."

"What?" I ask.

"I saw you at Adoration, when the Rebellious Ones first took action. I was afraid when Lucifer threw that spear and wounded God. I dropped to my knees and prayed. Then I saw you moving through the melee, avoiding swipes and blows as you made your way to God's side." She moved closer and reached for my hands, gently touching them. "You

pressed these hands to the wound in God's side, halting the flow of blood. I saw how you caught the drops of His blood in that cup."

My hand is over her wound. When I take it away it is healed. Not even a scar remains. She smiles at me. "A miracle," I say.

The glow from the sacred relic attracts the guards. They are curious but they do not venture out from their posts. Instead they hold back the curious, keeping the mass of angels behind the gates.

More of Cael's group has joined us. I gently cover the chalice with the plate and cloth, tucking it back into my robes.

"You must hide that immediately," says Cael. "Take it far from here."

"That is what I was about to do," I explain.

"It's not safe here in Heaven," he says.

"Not with the Fallen Ones loose," adds another of his band.

"Where would you suggest?" I ask.

The azure eyes beside me speak. "The Earth," she says. "I know of a cave there, a place hidden inside a great mountain. It is a long path through rock, with underground streams and secret passageways. It will be safe and well protected there."

"Tell me how to find this place," I say, eager to start my quest.

She laughs. "What are you going to do? Go alone? You against the Fallen Ones? Take on the beasts of the Earth as well? Have you considered there may be other dangers beyond your comprehension?"

I had not thought of it. "I don't want to endanger anyone. This is my problem. I can't ask anyone to risk exposure to such things."

"You're a brave one," she says, nodding in approval. A light shines from behind her, but like the cup, its origin is from within her. It is a sign and I know I will accept her help. "Come," she says. "We have little time and we must act quickly if we are to succeed."

"The two of you alone are not enough," says one of the angels standing beside Cael. "We will come with you."

A tall angel walks towards us, joining us from the gates. Flanked by angels bearing weapons he stands before me. "I know you," he says.

"And I, you," I reply. "You are Nakriel, Guard of the Gates of the South Wind. Who is that with you?"

"Never mind. We saw the Light and came to investigate. Show me what you have there." He points to my waist.

I start to unravel it from its place of safety when an angel steps between us. "No," he says. "It's time to leave."

"Is it what I think it is?" asks Nakriel.

"The Grail," says the angel. "We're taking it to safety."

"It's safe here in Heaven," says Nakriel.

We look back towards the gates. Inside there is turmoil. Fighting continues with shouts and distant clangs of armor. Another devil is outcast, transformed and thrown into the pit. He scurries to find his brethren and the safety of the pack.

"Is it?" I say. I turn to my new companions. "Let's go."

Cael and his friend turn and I start to follow. Nakriel grabs my arm and looks me in the eye. "If you will not return to the safety of Heaven, let some of us go with you. You will need protection, guards of the fifth order to protect you and the holy relic." There are nods behind him, the murmur of agreement.

"But Michael will scold you for deserting your posts," I say.

"We do not serve Michael. We serve Heaven," says one of them.

Cael introduces himself. "We are Neutral Angels," he says. "We cannot side with either faction, and so we choose a Middle Way."

"We accept that," says the angel beside Nakriel.

"We also do not like violence," says the angel with Cael. "Respect our way and you are welcome to join us."

"Very well," says Nakriel. He motions to the angels behind him. One steps forward to speak for them. "We are at your command," he says. "We are gate angels and guards, but also Neutral Angels. Let us travel with you as protectors and watchers."

I look at this group, significant in numbers now. The Neutral Angels are of all types and orders: Cherubim, Seraphim, Archangels, and even guardian angels. I recognize some of them: Nirgal, the protector, Dara of the rivers, and Israfel, angel of poetry. All are eager to help.

"I must return and man the gate, says Nakriel. "But I will not hold back any angels who wish to join you."

I address them all. "It will be dangerous," I say. "Earth presents challenges for which we may not be prepared, and the journey through the Firmament is not without peril." None retreat from my words. I secure the cup to my belt again feeling uplifted, this burden now shared between us.

I look at the lovely angel beside me, azure eyes surrounded by light from within.

"I am Holly," she says. "Time is short and disaster is upon us. We must go."

I feel a tingle. I reach out and hold her hand. She smiles, bearing her teeth as she moves closer, vicious canines that begin to rain drool upon my shoulder like a swollen waterfall. I try to let go of her hand but I cannot. I look down and watch as our fingers fuse, our skin turns blotchy red, covered thick with sores and open pustules.

I scream but I have no mouth. In its place is some kind of mutated fusion of genitals, both male and female. Holly roars, her pointed ears moving in concert to catch the sound of a distant wail, the mating call of another of our pack. We have fused together into some kind of beast, two misshapen heads that share the same body. I can't control the limbs, trapped as a helpless lump on her shoulder.

We run, leaping over the precipice into the mists, falling ever downward towards our fate, toward a distant roar that will lead us to the Fallen Ones.

29. To Rule in Heaven

We tumble down through the mists, disoriented and confused. I look at my daughter who is falling beside me. She is horrified. I shout, "That's not how it happened," but I have no mouth and she hears only my muffled cries.

We hit something flat and solid. My fused body dissolves and I am lying prone on the ground, my jaw aching from the impact. There is dirt in my mouth and I spit it out. My daughter lies beside me. "Are you all right?" I ask, surprised that I can use my voice. I shake her gently.

She opens her eyes and sees me, lets out a scream.

"It's okay. It's me," I say.

There is laughter in the background and I recognize it. "Yes, it's okay," says a familiar voice, laughter continuing like so much unwanted noise.

"What are you doing here?" I ask. "These are my memories."

There is anger in the voice now. "And they are incorrect," he says. "I'm here to see that you get it right."

"Oh, yes," I say. "And that fused beast thing. What was that?"

Laughter. "Just having some fun, brother," he says. "Weren't you ever curious, what kind of creature you would have become had you chosen to side with me?"

"Surely nothing as horrific as that," I say.

"Oh, no?" he says. He grabs my arm and pulls me up to standing, holding it next to his. "I gave you the same skin as I have. Something wrong with the complexion?"

"And the genitals?"

"You never were much of a talker," he says. "Figured it would be a better use of an orifice." He turns his back to me, chuckling, ignoring my comments and comebacks. My daughter now holds his attention. "Greetings," he says. "We've met briefly. September 11, New York City? Do you remember?"

She nods nervously.

"Did you enjoy your visit to the big city? Daddy take you sightseeing?"

"Stop," I say. "Leave her alone."

He turns, angered. "You be quiet, or I will stuff your mouth with genitals again." He turns back toward her, cooing with sweetness. "I want to visit with my niece."

"Uncle Lucifer?" she asks. "You look different than the last time I saw you."

"The devil doth take on a pleasing form," I say.

He ignores me.

"What are you doing here?" she asks.

"Your Father is not the only caretaker of memories," he says. "Also, he is not always accurate. I'm here to see he gets the story straight. After all, you deserve to hear the truth."

"No matter how many versions of it you may conjure," I say.

"Aren't you curious?" he says to her. "You already know that there can be many perspectives, many ways to look at the same thing. Inside your Father's memory you heard angels debate and not all of them agreed with your Father or with me for that matter. And I know you. You are your Father's child. You want to experience things with your own eyes and ears and form your own opinions based on observation. Aren't you curious about the other side of this story?"

"A little," she says.

He looks at me and smiles, then turns back to her.

"Wonderful," he says. He puts his hand behind his back and suddenly there is an apple in it. He presents it to her. "All you have to do it take a bite of this apple."

"What?" she asks.

"I grew it especially for you," he says. "It contains my memories. All you have to do is take a bite."

She looks nervously at me.

"Oh, ignore him," he says. "Your Father has nothing to do with this. It's your choice. Free will and all."

I can see she wants it. I wonder if, were I not here, would she reach for it now?

She answers my silent question. I watch her grab it from his hand and bite down. The skin breaks with a crunch and juice flows out of the corner of her mouth. She wipes it on her sleeve and I see a stain that turns dark. It forms a tiny, irregular shaped window on her arm and I see images move inside the stain. She takes another bite. Her eyes widen and she stares into the distance mesmerized. The apple slips from her hand.

He picks up the apple and wipes the dirt off with his cloak. He takes a bite and smiles. "They are delicious memories," he says, offering me the apple. "You may also want a bite. That is, if you want to be with her." He takes another bite.

She is a somnambulist, asleep and dreaming his memories. I take the apple from his hand, angry that he has tricked me once again. I huff at him, "To see the details of your demise? Wouldn't miss it." I take a big bite and chew.

It's delicious and he smiles.

"In case you haven't noticed, I have yet to meet my demise," he sighs. "Heaven may not be my kingdom, but I rule many lands unknown to God." He turns to her innocent, sleeping form. "Okay. Let's pick up where Daddy left off, shall we?"

And we slip into a dream.

30. Sour Apple

We are back in the past in Lucifer's great hall, the lofty palace from whence he will rule. The faithful are assembled. His legions number in the hundreds of thousands yet they seem to fit comfortably in this mountain retreat. There is fighting outside, practice for the coming battle, but most remain in the hall clamoring and shouting for direction from their leader.

His throne is high, the dais elevated. He has had it raised since the last time I was here. I check my belt, glad to find that the chalice is not with me. This would be the worst place to bring it, and its absence confirms my suspicions that this is another of my brother's elaborate illusions.

Yet it feels so real. I hear the mulling of his disciples; I sense that their loyalty is waning. They grow restless, and I see their zeal for battle outweighs their restraint. There is a commotion in the back of the hall as a contingency arrives: spies from the gates of Heaven. The crowd parts and allows the newcomers to come forward to greet their commander.

I am shocked to see Mbriel at the head of this group. He is not their prisoner but their leader. He steps forward, prostrating before Lucifer.

"They have cast our brethren over the precipice at the gates of Heaven," he says.

"The cowards," shouts Lucifer. "Unable to find us, they have taken revenge against our wounded."

"Yes," says Beelzebub, his second in command who stands beside him on the dais. "They fear us. We have shown them that we have the strength and the will to take action."

Mbriel steps aside to allow another to speak, a member of the Order of Dominion. "What about that Sword that Michael has?" asks Paimon. "I saw The Sword cut limbs free from bodies. It has the very power of God within it."

"Fool," yells Lucifer. "Any sword can cut. God has no power. Did you not see him bleed? What bleeds can be destroyed."

"And what then?" comes a voice from the back of the hall.

"Then we rule Heaven in our own way," he shouts. "We will not have to bow to Man or to any lesser creature. Heaven is for angels and it should be ruled by angels."

And who better to rule, than I?" he mutters. Beelzebub snickers.

Mbriel's party steps back as another group of soldiers arrive. The crowd in the great hall of evil parts once again, allowing them space to approach Lucifer's throne. They bow and bend to one knee before him.

These acts of subservience please him and he smiles graciously as they rise.

As their commander steps forward I recognize him as Balam, also of the Order of Domination. So many have fallen under my brother's spell! I wonder how many of this Order have given themselves over to Lucifer. There are great voids in the organization of Heaven.

"Good news, my lord," reports Balam. "They do not know where we are."

Lucifer smiles. "Do you mean God, in all his omnipotence, cannot see us?" He laughs. "Perhaps time spent with Man in the relative darkness of the Earth has blinded his Heavenly vision."

"There is more, my lord," says the commander. "God has ordered our expulsion from Heaven. He has charged Michael, promoting him to the greatest of Archangels, trusting him with the Sword of Fire."

"Michael," murmurs Lucifer, stroking his beard.

"Michael has organized others. They conspire against up. He has allied with Gabriel, Raphael, and Sachiel. Our spies report that he has but to ask, and the rest of the Archangels will join him."

"Why does this news not surprise me?" says Lucifer, rising from his throne and moving toward the edge of the hall. Outside and below he scans the distant realms of Heaven. "We have the advantage at this time," he says. "They know not where we hide, so in the midst of this confusion we must plan a strike against them."

"But what about the Sword of Fire?" asks Balam. "How can we hope to prevail against such a weapon?"

"While Michael and his hunting party are busy wandering about, brandishing his Sword of Power, we will strike at the very heart of what they should be protecting."

"Do you mean…" the commander begins, guessing Lucifer's thoughts.

"Precisely, my clever friend," he says. "I see I have chosen my leaders well. You are blessed with exceptional intelligence." He put his hand on the angel's shoulder. "God is vulnerable now. He lies blinded and wounded, wallowing in misery and fear. He is so weak that he cannot even sit upon his throne. He has to lie on his side. We must finish the job, now, while we have the chance."

"But what about The Sword?" comes a voice from the gallery. Shouts follow. There is fear in the ranks.

Beelzebub steps forward. "You let me worry about The Sword," he says. "With my best men I will sortie against Michael, leading him on a merry chase through Heaven. He will not catch us, but he will follow relentlessly. Perhaps he will drop in exhaustion from carrying that heavy weapon." He laughs.

Lucifer nods in agreement and turns to Balam. "And meanwhile, you and your men will come with me. You can even lead the strike against God."

Balam accepts the honor nervously. "Thank you, My Lord."

Lucifer lays a gentle hand on his new pet and stands before his men. His voice elevates, filling the hall with his words. "It will be God Almighty and His followers that are cast down from Heaven. Let Him rule on Earth with Man at His side. It will be a fitting end for Him."

"Yes, but what about Michael and that Sword?" says the voice in the crowd again.

"Michael will ultimately come to God's rescue, and it is then that we will bargain for The Sword. I will offer him God in exchange for the ultimate weapon of power. Once I have The Sword of Fire, God and Michael will be banished, never to return, and Heaven will be ours."

There are cheers from the hall as the Fallen Ones join in support of Lucifer and Beelzebub's plan.

31. Armory of Darkness

There is a commotion from the back of the hall as a new group enters. Once again, the crowd parts to let them pass. At the head of the group is a young, strong angel flanked by two others, giants in stature. The giants carry something long between them, a bundle wrapped and covered in stout cloth.

"We bring it, my lord," says the strong young angel. "We managed to wrest it from the grasp of one of His defending angels." The giants put down the bundle and open the cloth, revealing many spears bound together. They release the ropes holding them and they clank against the floor. "We also forged these weapons from metal extracted from a falling star. They are the strongest known. These giants with me were to be teachers, tasked with teaching Man the ways of civilization. Their opinions on Man are similar to our own and so they agree to help us. It is their skills that stoked the fires and created these weapons," he says. He turns to the rest of the congregation. "We are only sorry that there is not enough metal for each of you to have a magic weapon."

Dark angels rush forward, each bent on grabbing one of the weapons for their own. "Hold fast," commands Lucifer. "Since these weapons are few in number we must use them carefully. Beelzebub and his men should have the first pick, in case they encounter Michael. It is only fitting that they be equally armed."

"We will take only a few," says Beelzebub. "My band and I are expendable, but great is your gesture and your concern for our safety, Lucifer." As he reaches for the spears, another wrapped bundle inside the pile is revealed. "What's this?" he asks.

The young angel nods and the giants pick up the bundle and unwrap it with careful ceremony. Inside is a single spear. The shaft glistens and the tip of the spear reveals a dark stain upon close inspection. The giants hold the open bundle forward presenting it to Lucifer. The spear rests on the cloth, as if they are not worthy enough to touch such an object. "This is for you, my lord. It is the very spear that struck the side of God," he says.

Lucifer's mouth drops as he reaches out to accept the weapon. "How did you get this?" he asks.

"We took it from the field of battle. When God pulled it from His wound, He cast it aside. We retrieved it during our retreat. The shaft was broken but we have fashioned a new one from the star metal and mounted the tip upon it."

"So the blood has been purged from the tip?" he asks.

"Burned in the fires of transformation," states a giant. "But there is still a stain on the tip."

Lucifer balances the spear in his hand, hefting the weight and pretending to aim and throw it. "It feels so light, yet it has mass," he says.

"It too was forged from a special fire. Deep within the Earth burns an eternal fire, molten metal purified at the source of incredible heat and pressure. At great risk we retrieved just enough metal to contribute to this weapon."

"It is a fine weapon," says Lucifer, smiling. He raises it over his head and the air around him hisses with power. The hall is filled with triumphant shouts, promising glory and allegiance to Lucifer and his cause. "The reign of God in Heaven is over," he shouts, holding in his hands a weapon truly equal to Michael's. "Once we have cast them from Heaven, we shall descend to Earth and rescue our brethren, returning them to the glory of Heaven. Then we will fashion a kingdom more to our liking, and one day rule both Heaven and Earth from here on high."

"Lord Lucifer," says a scout. "Michael has left God's side along with most of the Archangels. Gabriel travels with him. I have seen Hizkiel, his standard bearer, side by side with Michael's. They have armed themselves heavily, eager to do battle in the name of the Lord. They do not fear you, Lord Lucifer. They are driven by vengeance."

Lucifer turns this thought over in his mind. "Vengeance, hmmmm…" He smiles.

"They underestimate your power," says Azkeel, leader of the two hundred. "They forget you are also an Archangel."

"True," says Rahab, giving testimonial. "God tried to destroy me, and He was unable!"

"Many of us are Archangels," says Azazel. "We are skilled in the techniques of battle."

"Yes," says Lucifer. "Both sides seem equal in their abilities and their desire to destroy each other. We have practiced for battle and planned long enough." He stands defiantly, his staff raised high. It hums with power, static electricity building a charge. His voice carries the same energy. "It is time. Michael marches out to meet us. Let us not disappoint him."

A mighty shout goes out. The hall becomes loud and resonant with the cries of battle. How can God not hear this noise?

Beelzebub's men are first to assemble, first to leave. From his spear he affixes a banner for all to see, a flag of honor to fight for. The flag is red and black, with images on it that change as it flutters. He hands it to his standard bearer, then calls his captains to his side: Azkeel, Urian, Drsmiel, and Euronymous, the last a leader of his special detachment.

"Euronymous, you and your flying brigade of scouts are vital to the plan," he says. "You must capture Michael's attention and draw him out. Let him chase you. Work in concert with Azkeel."

With the mention of his name the Captain of the two hundred smiles. "We are at your command," he says, tapping is chest. "What would you have us do?"

Beelzebub shakes his head sadly. "I'm not sure if you are up to the task," he says.

"We are," says Azkeel. "Try us."

"Can you cry like cowards? Run with fear? Retreat with all your heart?"

"What?"

"Because this is what you must do. Lead them away, far from this hall and from our main force. Tire them out. Amble across the plains, change direction, scatter in disarray. They will quicken their pace thinking you retreat and this will help tire them out. When you think they have had enough, lead them to us."

Azkeel sniggers, a demonic laugh that makes Beelzebub smile. He continues. "Yes. Lead them to us where they will meet their demise at our hands. When the moment is right, we will strike against them. Then you can join us and turn against them in battle."

Eronymous nods in understanding and laughs. Azkeel's eyes glow with fire. Beelzebub continues, predicting a terrible future for his foes. "There will be no escape. Michael and Gabriel will be expelled, along with the disillusioned defenders, gilded gate guards, and confused cretins who remain. Victory will be ours, Lucifer has seen it. We will clear the way for him to confront God in one final contest and then Heaven will be ours forever."

He nods to his standard bearer who waves the flag. Horns blare, assembling the loyal foot soldiers of discord. A shout goes out and I wonder again why God cannot hear this terrible noise. His band pours down from Lucifer's palace like sand falling off the mountainside. Above this advancing horde circle winged messengers, Eronymous and his band who scout the surrounding areas in search of the enemies of Lucifer.

My brother is ecstatic, his look triumphant. He gazes on with childish glee, his heart light with celebration. He watches the horde thunder into battle.

In the confusion I touch my daughter gently, her spirit beside me witnessing these events. "We can stay here and watch this insanity, or we can get on with my version. There really is nothing to see here, nothing to taste but anger. Come, let me show you what love can do."

Lucifer catches my plan but too late. The room fades and we hear my brother shouting angrily for our return.

32. The Descent of Pain

We have returned to my stream of memories. I mutter a small prayer of protection to keep us safe from my brother's influence. The drama proceeds true to the past, free of Lucifer's illusions. And once again I witness my history, unable to alter it, unable to comment.

We stand on the precipice, Holly and I flanked by a small band of Neutral Angels. Cael has organized his group. They are eager for this mission. True to his word, Nakriel has let others pass through the gate. We are joined by Vassago, Rochel and Nilaihah. They bring more with them, eager angels sworn to neutrality. Holly has quested with some of them before and she welcomes them to our growing band.

I wrap the chalice in cloth, the plate on top protecting its precious contents. With rope and tassel I secure it to my belt.

"This way," says Holly, pointing down and into the mists. "We will have to scale it by hand. It's slow but safer."

"Why can't we fly or glide?" I ask.

"The air becomes thick as we get closer to Earth. Once we pass through the clouded mists, there will be a Firmament. Although we can move through it, it is difficult. It can even be disorienting, easy to get lost. Only by clinging to the wall of the precipice can you keep your balance and your orientation."

I take a deep breath and remember what the Firmament was like in the beginning. There were no crossed lines of prayers or traveling angels. It was new and unexplored. Only a few Angels had gone there, mostly on their way to Earth and the Garden of Eden.

Holly continues. "Crossing the Firmament will be difficult. We will have to crawl at times. Our wings are too fragile to swim through that region, the air too dense and thick to fly. Not that it can't be done; it just takes conditioning and strength. It's like learning how to swim in water, only much more difficult. Then there is the molting disease."

"I have heard of it," I say. "I know some angels who suffer from it."

"Don't worry," says Vassago beside her. "Some of us have made this journey before. Just follow our instructions. We will guide you."

"Thank you," I say. "Any journey is better with a guide." I turn to Holly. "You've made this trip before? How many times?"

"More than I can remember," she says. "And you?"

"I went on several missions with my brother. We traveled in a sacred vessel and were protected from the elements. It's a lot different than walking." I look over the edge and stare down into the mists. "I'm glad you are with me and I am grateful for your help." I grip the chalice tightly as I push myself over the precipice and onto a small foot trail that hugs the mountainside.

"Stop!" One of the angels produces a rope. "We must bind ourselves together into teams. That way if one of us slips or falls, the others will be able to suspend them until we can restore order to our descent."

"Good idea," I say, and that is how I came to be bound beside Holly.

The way down is perilous and we move in slow silence. She travels ahead of me and I carefully follow her footsteps. The trail narrows quickly to the width of a single footprint. We rely on each other to make safe passage. The sacred relic remains tightly tied to my belt despite the danger. I think of how the return trip will be easier when it is safely hidden and I no longer have to carry it.

We pick our way across the sheer rock face. I look down and see steep cliffs that disappear into distant grey mists. This continues for some time until we reach a flat area with a wide series of switchbacks. We stop to remove the ropes and secure them for later use. After a brief rest, we continue down the trail, the width allowing us to walk side by side. I take the opportunity to talk to Holly.

"I heard you mention Neutral Angels," I say. "Can you tell me more about them and who they are?"

"We are the Neutral Angels," she says, "And we do not take sides in this battle."

"But, isn't that a choice, too?" I ask, "By not taking sides, do you not choose a side after all? You actually have your own side, a Middle Way, I thought I heard it called. Perhaps there are three sides to Heaven."

"Three is a sacred number," she says.

We continue in silence for a while. The mists grow dense to cover us like a shroud. We stop and affix the ropes again. "We will not be able to see each other during this part of the journey even though we are close. Keep tension on the rope and follow my lead."

"How do you know which way to go?" I ask.

"There are signs. The trail is marked but you have to know what to look for. Just be careful," she says, drawing me close despite the length of rope between us. "Hold tight to the Grail."

"Why do you call it a Grail?" I ask.

"That is the correct term for a receptacle which holds the blood of God. Properly, it is the Holy Grail," she says.

"I have not heard this word Grail. It is new to me. Where did you hear it?" I ask.

She pauses a moment, her face scrunched in thought, and with no answer coming, says, "It just is. It's called a Grail and that's the word for it."

"Oh," I say. "How did you know about it?"

"From a story that many of us heard when we were young. The Rebellious Ones and their Fall from Grace has been predicted for some time," she says.

"Really?" I ask, surprised at this news. I had suspicions, but I would not voice these thoughts to any others, especially my brother. "I've heard rumors, stories told in whispers that I didn't want to believe, but this is news to me. You say it was predicted?"

She begins to explain. "When God created the first angels, as the story goes, He knew that they were flawed and would eventually be tempted and fall. That is why He created grace, but for some reason known only to Him, he withheld this grace from certain angels."

"Why would he do that?" I ask.

"As I said," she continues, "Only God knows His reasons."

Now we enter a mist, so thick that the very breath of it causes my lungs and my body to feel heavy. I begin to ache, and Holly senses my despair. "Don't try to talk. It is difficult. We must press onward," she says. "We will quickly pass through this mist and into the Firmament. Steady your breathing and move carefully, for it is easy to become distracted here."

The air is thicker and the trail narrows again. I can barely see my feet through the mist. I sense a great precipice at my side. The Grail scrapes against the rock on the other side as I cling to it. I feel it coming loose and I steady myself, one hand trying to hold the wall while the other secures the chalice. The air chills me and my wings began to stir involuntarily. I start to teeter.

Holly reaches out and steadies me, taking the Grail from my grasp until I regain my balance. My wings continue to flutter and she marks the signs of fatigue in me.

"You don't want to lose this," she says, securing it to her belt. "Your wings flutter, trying to adjust to these conditions. Mine did the same on my first journey."

I look into her eyes and see that glow again, this time directed at me. I feel her strength and courage build within me. She is indeed a special angel.

But I am weak. She pulls us onward, the rope urging me to follow like a tethered animal.

"I don't know if I could have made this journey without you or your companions", I say.

"Probably not," she says. "There are angels still missing from the early explorations."

"How many times have you been this way?" I ask.

"This is my fourth time going by foot. The last few times I drifted down on thick currents of air. It took some strength."

"I've noticed," I say, shy at pointing it out. "You have beautiful, large wings."

She smiles. "Soon you will too."

33. Dense is the Firmament

The way grows narrow again and talk is difficult. I hear the sounds of the Neutral Angels following in my footsteps as I have been following in Holly's. The angels ahead of me remain steady, it is the ones behind that I worry about.

There are moans and complaints and I am not alone in my suffering. The air becomes unbearably thick, each breath weighing heavy on my chest. There are spasms and I try to concentrate but I am helpless to stop my wings from fluttering. Holly senses my trouble, turns and holds me in firm embrace. The warmth of her beside me, the grasp of her arms, it imparts control in the face of chaos. It steadies my resolve and I find the strength to continue.

There is no orientation in this mist, no indication that we cross any boundary that separates Heaven from Earth. Breath is labored, steps painfully slow, and the spasms frequent. There is pressure inside my head causing unexplained lapses in my thinking. I can't seem to concentrate.

The groans behind me are motivation. They keep me moving. If I stop I become a stone in the trail and they will be unable to go around me. A tug on the rope reminds me that forward is the only way, and so I reach out to find a new handhold and take yet another nervous step.

Just as things reach new levels of unbearable, we emerge into a murky light. The mists disappear and we descend out of the clouds. The slope is no longer steep, the path wide. Soon we gently set foot upon flat ground. It is not a great space, but a level area next to the high wall and the trail that leads back towards Heaven. There is an overlook across from the cliff. We are on high ground above a sweeping valley that lay far below, green patches of bright vegetation resting upon a vast, brown, rock-stubble plain.

"You're looking south," she says. "That bright patch is the Garden of Eden in the distance, and over there," she points southeast to a distant range of cliffs, "that is a barren land filled with harsh winds and scant vegetation."

We remove the ropes that bind us together. Dedicated angels coil them and stow them away. We will no longer need them but I feel uncomfortable without the security of Holly tethered beside me. Other angels continue to join us, descending from the murky Firmament that still hangs close above. They remove their ropes, forming small groups that become lively with chatter. A restless few scout the path ahead as well as our surroundings. They return and report their findings.

"No sign of the Fallen Ones here," one of them says. "At least not in the immediate vicinity."

"Oh, no? Look here," says an angel. She points to a mass on the ground. We gather about, spying shards of cloth on a damp patch of mountain grass. There are dark feathers spread about, signs of recent molting, and odd patches of scales and skin. Footprints litter the ground, some not so angelic. "Signs of the Fallen Ones. They have been here. It's likely more will follow as they are expulsed from Heaven."

I feel uneasy. We begin to glance about nervously.

"Do you think they saw us coming and hid?" asks Nirgal the Protector.

"We told you," repeats one of the scouts. "They are not in the vicinity. We have searched well."

"Keep a vigilant eye, just in case," says Basus, one of the angels from the gate. "These Fallen Ones are tricky, filled with deception."

"They caught us by surprise once, but never again," says Nirgal.

"We can't let them get to the Grail," says Cael.

"Defend the Grail," comes a chorus of shouts.

I turn to Holly. "The Grail must be secured," she says. "You should carry this." She unties the cup from her waist and hands it to me.

"Thank you for keeping it safe," I say. "I don't know if I could trust anyone else with this task."

"I never thought I would feel such a burden from so small an object," she says. "The group is right. We should press onward."

"Which way then?" I ask.

She points the opposite way we came. "Over there," she says. "The path between the stones leads down the steep side of the mountain, there we must traverse a narrow ridge to a small restriction that will take us to the inside of this mountain."

"And then we are done?" I ask, eager to make a quick end to this adventure and return to Heaven.

"Oh, no," she laughs. "That's where the real danger begins."

"What do you mean by that?"

Before she can answer we are interrupted. An angel flutters her wings in frustration. "Why can't we fly?" she asks. "Wouldn't it be easier to get there by flying?"

Another angel takes flight. "Some of us can," he says. "But there are dangerous winds, dense air, and unexpected pockets of clouds. The cliff side is prone to whirlwinds. You'll need lots of practice."

My spasms have stopped. I give it a try and rise a few inches above the ground.

"Very good," says Holly.

"We need a rear guard," says Jekusial. "In case the Fallen Ones should try to block our return to Heaven."

"A wise precaution," says Kzuial. "But instead of standing guard openly, maybe we should secret ourselves in rocks and crevices and conceal our presence and numbers."

"Yes, yes," agrees Jekusial. "Kzuial is an angelic guard and trained in security, defense, and protection. He should know."

"I'll stay with you and guard," says Basus.

"Me, too," echoes Jekusial.

Pachdiel and Zerachiel, two of the gate guards who joined us on this mission, volunteer to stay as well. "We also have knowledge of security," one of them says.

And so it is done. The rest of us, a smaller band than we had started with, begin the journey down the tight and narrow path between the stones.

34. Cleft in the Rock

Jagged rock lines hug both sides of the trail. The mists are behind me, yet I feel claustrophobic, my breathing heavy and labored again. The rock rubble underfoot makes each step slippery. One of our party has already been injured in a fall.

The Sacred Mountain rumbles, the walls of rock around us shake as if they will collapse at any moment. Fear strikes my heart, soon to be compounded. We round a curve and the space beside us opens up into a high ledge beside a monstrous pit of fire. A fetid blast of heat rises, clinging to my robes like hot oil. I begin to sweat and my hand fumbles for grip. The mountain rumbles again. The ground shakes and I see pieces of a nearby wall crack and fall into the lake of fire. The sound is deafening. Despite the heat, a sudden chill consumes me.

"This way," says Holly, pointing towards a shelf that leads to the right.

"Should we use the ropes?" I ask.

She shakes her head. "No time," she says. "The way is quick, and if we hurry, luck may be with us. We may only lose a few, and the less time spent near the lake of fire, the better."

"Does the mountain always rumble so?" asks another.

"No, just in spots," she says. "It did not rumble at our point of descent where we emerged from the Firmament, and if we pass through this narrow way we will quickly find another place of safety. These short rumbles build until they are compounded, then they let loose with rampant fury. For our own safety we must keep moving before the next big one."

The path is narrow and we fight the urge to push past each other in panic. On one side there is towering jagged rock and the other empty space, dropping sheer and steep into the lake of fire. The heat wafts up and singes my left side, but I keep moving. I hold the Grail tightly, consumed by the fear that I will drop it into the lake and cause our mission to fail. We huddle along; watching carefully our step, for each placement must be cautious and balanced. There is a prayer on each of our lips as the mountain rumbles once again.

I follow closely behind Holly as she picks her way across the ledge. She looks behind occasionally to *check on us, and it is good to see her concern for our safety.*

My feet begin to burn with the heat. We are all walking on hot coals. There is a low rumble and rock falls behind us. "How much farther?" I ask, the sound of boiling rock deafening my words.

"Not far," she says, her speech short. The temperature in the air forces shallow breaths as waves of heat and fire rise from below. "There," she shouts, pointing ahead. "Hurry."

I can not see beyond her or what she is pointing at. Smoke clouds my eyes and I lose sight of her. The ledge suddenly takes an abrupt right into a cleft in the rock. I panic, caught off balance, my worst fears making me step forward and off the ledge as it turns. She grabs my arm as I am about to tumble into the abyss, gently pulling me towards a narrow fissure, barely a crack that could contain us both at one time. I watch her duck under a narrow constriction and disappear into a dark hole in the back of the crevice.

Here I have no guide for what I need to do. What lies in the darkness? My mind imagines strange things that I cannot describe. Already I have seen things beyond my ken. I push myself on, trusting she who has led me truthfully.

It is cool in that darkness and my scorched body begins to feel eased of pain. "Over here," says a soft voice next to me. I feel a gentle hand at my side as she leads me to a nearby wall. "Stand here. Your eyes will adjust to the darkness after a short time and you will be able to see again."

She goes back towards the entrance to help others who are still emerging through that dim hole. Patiently she guides them to a place of safety beside me where they strain to adapt to these new conditions. My eyes adjust to the shadows. Images dance across my mind as the glow from the lake of fire dimly filters in through the hole. We are in a cave, a small room no bigger than a country church.

"Rest for a moment," she says. "And watch a miracle."

We wait patiently, I, for one, welcoming the rest. I sit on the cool stone floor of the cavern and eye the surroundings in the pale light. There are shadows in the rock and it smells dark and funny, unlike anything I have experienced. There is a draft against my wings as a hot, humid wind blows by. It carries the scent of something moist and unfathomable. I inhale deeply, sniffing out loud.

"It is the smell of the Earth," she says. "I can describe it no other way. It is the scent of the rock and the water and the fire and air all combined. They are the elements that God used to create this place."

"I can't see," says a voice in the darkness.

"Your eyes will adjust," she says. "Be patient."

I wonder when we will see the promised miracle, but I am not disappointed. My eyes adjust and I see the others, glowing softly at first, but getting brighter with each breath they take. I realize that most of the light has not been coming from outside, but from within us. It is beautiful; the glow strengthens and brightens the cavern with radiance, as if we each had donned a shimmering cloak.

"I've never seen anything like it," says Israfel, the Angel of Poetry.

"It is the Light from Within," says Holly. "The Light that guides us like an inner beacon can also shine outside us. The purity of our angelic state makes this light appear. We do not notice it in Heaven because it is so bright there, shining with God's love, but here in the darkness, that piece of the Creator within us all shines through."

35. The Guest From Hell

There is noise and motion at the entrance of the cavern, the narrow fissure that leads to the outside ledge above the lake of fire. We glow with the Light from Within as we rest with our backs to the stone walls. Opposite the fissure the cave narrows and continues into darkness.

Holly helps an angel joining us from the ledge. "Are you the last one?" she asks.

"Yes," answers my daughter.

My daughter? Where has she been all this time? And why doesn't Holly recognize her? Something is off. My daughter has not been born yet. But if this is memory, things are still not right. My mind is out of focus and I am confused, lost momentarily between my memories and my struggle with reality.

Next to me an angel is asleep, another odd thing. Angels do not sleep, as we are continually refreshed and energized by God's love. I wonder. Could I also be asleep?

Then I look around and notice that everyone is asleep, including Holly. Their eyes are closed as they gently breathe. Only my daughter and I are awake. There is a disturbance at the fissure and we both turn towards the entrance.

"Room for one more?" he asks as he comes through the opening. "Ah, it's cozy in here, isn't it?" He looks around and makes himself at home, removing his cloak and hat.

My daughter is surprised. "Uncle Lucifer?" she says.

He smiles.

"What are you doing here?" I ask.

"You ran away" he says. "I'm just catching up, my darling niece. Besides, I'm here to answer your questions."

"We're dealing with my memories now," I say.

"Yes," he says. "The sacred Grail mission, I see. So this is what it was like. I see you still have the relic."

He reaches out to grab the chalice from my hip but I am a ghost. His hand passes right through me.

Not what he expected.

Or I.

Lucifer regains his composure. "Memories," he says. "Half the story, as I pointed out, tainted with false perception, wrapped in personal commentary. My niece has questions that you cannot answer. Don't you, my sweet?" He turns his attention and his charms toward her.

"Yes," she says.

I scowl. They both ignore me.

"Ah, a child's curiosity," he remarks. "Now where were we, my sweet? Yes, I was in the middle of answering your questions, not his, wasn't I?"

"I have lots of them," she says.

"Fire away," he says. "Anything."

"Your second in command was Beelzebub. I thought that Beelzebub was just another name for you."

He chuckles. "You're clever to pick up on that," he says. He turns to me momentarily. "It runs in the family, doesn't it?" He clears his throat and turns back to her. "Actually, Beelzebub is Satan who is also Lucifer who is also Mephistopheles who is me who is, well, I can go on and on, but you get the idea. Have you ever heard the phrase that evil has many faces?"

"Yes," she says.

He expands, his color changing, a giant red monster that threatens to take up the entire cavern. His face twists, an odd contortion that gives him three heads with a thousand faces. They hiss and growl at us and she screams.

He reverts to his former image, shrinking back into kind old Uncle Lucifer. "Sorry," he says, chuckling. "Couldn't resist giving you a little scare. Like playing 'Boo' with you when you were a baby, only a little more grown up."

She regains her composure and smiles nervously at him.

"Yes, many faces," he says. "I have powers, some I have never revealed. One of them is the ability to be in many places at once. I am just as omnipresent as God. I can be two, three, four, even dozens of people at the same time. I can see things from many perspectives."

"And yet, your omnipresence has not revealed the location of the Grail to you," I say.

"The Grail is missing," he says. "Nobody knows where it is."

"Don't be so certain," I say.

My daughter senses the tension building between us. "So when you were Beelzebub agreeing with Lucifer, then you were really just agreeing with yourself," she says.

"Yes," I say. "Manipulating the crowd like some cheap politician. How much of that crowd was made up of you, admiring yourself in your many forms?"

"I'm answering her questions now," he says. "Please hold all yours until later."

"It just proves that you have to think for yourself," I say to her.

"Comments, too," he says. "Please hold them until later. No more interruptions." He turns away from me, finished. "Back to you, my sweet."

"How did you lead the attack against Michael and God at once?" she asks. "What was it like being both Beelzebub and Lucifer at the same time? How did you manage to control two armies?"

"Patience," he says. "So many questions. It is perhaps best if I show you." He reaches behind his back and produces the apple, fresh and crisp except for the few bites taken out of it from before.

He smiles and hands it to her. To my surprise, she does not hesitate and instead takes a bite and passes it to me.

"We're coming to the best part, aren't we," he says, waiting for me to take a bite.

36. The Red Fruit

One bite and I feel it stir within me, the memories held at bay by the façade of a children's story.

"I don't know if I want to see this," she says.

I feel sick to my stomach.

"Too late," says my brother. "Welcome to my world."

I begin to sweat cold, images boiling up from inside of me. She sees it too, the horror beginning to play out before us. Like an automaton, I try to speak. This is my world of terror and dark visions, shadow memories of the war. I have shielded her from this for so long.

Her lip quivers and she tries to cover her ears, but it is futile. Even when I close my eyes I see my brother's memories. We can do nothing but bear mute witness.

Beelzebub leads his men down the mountain and they spread like locusts across the foothills that lie before the Plains of Heaven. He motions to Euronymous, commanding his special unit. They take flight in a flutter of wings and weapons. They fan out, searching the horizon for movement, anxious to make contact with the enemy.

Euronymous signals Azkeel, and the two hundred break away from Beelzebub's main group. They lag behind the flock, eyes to the sky for direction, feet to the ground to make dust. With the boisterous noise they create, it appears to be a large army on the move.

Beelzebub orders his remaining men to take up places of concealment. They huddle in crevices and crouch beneath rocks. Lying down flat they hide under cloaks that mimic the color and pattern of the ground. And from the great hall on high Lucifer waits and watches, ready with the reserves, knowing full well that they will be needed, that a time will come when he will have to commit all his forces.

Euronymous spies the approach of Michael and hears the heavenly heralds in the distance. The Sword is bright, a divine beacon that is conspicuous.

His second in command sees them too. He points and says, "They carry their standards and their weapons with confidence."

"I would call it arrogance, Tumael," says Euronymous. "The righteous possess a natural ability that makes them feel morally superior."

"It's so bright. I can hardly look at it. He must be blinding his own troops."

"Yes, it's difficult to see," says Euronymous. "A light like that could illuminate the darkness that surrounds Beelzebub and his men. Go and warn our leader. Meanwhile we will do our part." He nods to his angels in flight, then signals Azkiel and the troops below.

A whoop of noise goes up, cries of panic and fear. Euronymous and his men hover near the ground, flapping their wings beside the two hundred to stir the dust and add to the false impression that there are thousands on the plains.

From a distance Michael and his noble army of Archangels are deceived by this trick. "After them!" he shouts, pointing with the Sword of Fire. A beam of light shoots from the tip and brightens the sky around Euronymous. "There they are. Forward."

There is thunder from both camps, but as Michael rushes forward, Azkiel retreats. He follows true to the plan and together with Euronymous they begin the ploy of random movements, panic, dust clouds, and cries of cowardice.

"Brave warriors," says Michael. "They run from us like fearful children."

"They are fast for a large army," says Gabriel.

"Of course," says Michael. "We have them in retreat. We must continue to pursue them."

"But we are heavy with armor and divine weaponry," says Gabriel. "We'll never catch them."

"We must make the effort," he says. "We will chase them off the plains to the very precipice of Heaven. Sound the pursuit, Gabriel."

The mighty Archangel puts his horn to his lips and blows the sacred notes. The ranks form and the loyal angels hasten their pace. Wings flap in double time, battle armor clangs, and the heavy wheels of holy cannon grind against Heaven's flatlands.

Beelzebub hears the flourish and knows the meaning of Gabriel's message. "Fools," he whispers. "Do they not realize that this trumpet announces their every move and intent, even to us?"

"They are fanning out," says an observer, peering from behind a rock.

"Get down," cautions Beelzebub. "Stay out of sight. There is no need to look at them directly. Don't you know that our own scouts tell us their every move?"

They look up at a brigade of Lucifer's angels flying a safe distance away. They are banded in formations, making symbols and messages that hold meaning for Beelzebub. "That formation means they will lead them once more across the plain and then back into our midst for their final deliverance."

True to form, the Archangels follow the false clouds of the two hundred. They go far across the Plains of Heaven, out of sight from Beelzebub save for two moving clouds of dust in the distance. But then like a tornado, the twin clouds turn, growing thicker and larger as they move closer towards the hidden hoard.

"Ready the men," he says. "Brace yourselves for a storm." The evil general smiles watching his men take up hooks and knives and swords. There is stillness in the air, as if held stationary in time, and Heaven seems to stop all movement.

The two hundred thunder across their path, stomping their feet so hard that the rocks shake free of dust. Beelzebub nods to his leaders. The men are nervous and anxious for battle. "Be still," he whispers. "Wait for them to pass. The two hundred will turn and we will have them trapped between us."

Michael stops, raising his hand to halt his army. He holds The Sword level in his hand and closes his eyes. A green glow emanates from the blade, reaching out from The Sword like a beacon. It shines on the hillside exposing Beelzebub's forces. They glow yellow, their shapes revealed behind solid rocks and buried ground.

Gabriel sounds a flourish, one that Beelzebub recognizes as an alert. He pops his head up, and a mighty shout is heard from Michael's camp as they lift their swords and weapons for the Fallen Ones to see.

"Betrayed," said Beelzebub. "The light of that blasted Sword has given us away."

"You can't hide from the might of God," yells Michael.

Gabriel sounds the horn again, and the great armies of Heaven rise up and charge each other. In the air, powerful angels on both sides slam into each other with forces that knock them to the ground. The two hundred turn, cowardice no longer in their throats. The sound of metal ringing in the hills deafens the slash of swords against flesh. Shouts and screams fill the air.

Beelzebub calls for his flying angels to rain death from above. They load up, buckets harnessed to their waists, they take off moving heavy and slow in flight. Hovering above the center of Michael's lines, they drop buckets of molten fire. The army scatters in disarray. Angels scream in agony fighting to get away from falling globs of fire. Michael's forces split in two and Beelzebub's men take advantage to charge the weakened ranks.

Angels of Protection raise their arms, creating shields of pure white light which knit together and form a protective roof above the ground troops. The fire splatters against the invisible shield. Despite the protection, angels beneath it cringe with fear as the rain of fire bursts above them.

One of Michael's best, Vhnori, springs into action. A skilled archer, he loads his bow with sacred arrows thrice blessed with prayer. He kisses the tip of one and steps out from under the shield. Raising his aim skyward, he finds a target. The arrow flies from his bow and rips through an angel's wing, pinning it deep between the shoulder blades. The pot of fire falls from his hands as he reaches behind to pull the arrow out. Off balance and unable to fly, he falls to the ground where the pots tied to his waist explode in a ball of flame. Screaming, he curdles in the fire, burning as he twists in agony.

Again and again Vhnori's arrows find targets and the flames on the ground grow. Demon and angel are locked in combat beside the conflagration. The Angels of Protection try to maintain the shield but it falters. A section collapses, burying the fighters beneath rivers of fire. The screams drown out the sound of clashing metal as wounded and burning angels retreat.

Beelzebub hears the cries of terror. He raises his mighty staff, the banner now tattered and stained with the blood of battle. There are images of death fluttering in its folds. A bolt of lightning flies from the tip, reaching into the darkening sky above. Meteors began to fall, called down from the Heavens by his power, giant rocks of burning stone from which even the Angels of Protection cannot hide. They smash the remaining shelters, burying angels underneath tons of rock.

Michael is vigilant, aware of Beelzebub's action. He plunges forward, clashing his Sword into Beelzebub's staff and deflecting the lightning. It strikes the mountain above, setting off an avalanche of rock that causes all in its path to stop fighting and flee. Many are buried outright beneath hurling piles of stone. Others are maimed and fall crying to the ground grasping wounds and yelling for help. Before the smoke can clear, bands of evil minions, lesser Fallen Angels, set upon the rock piles, freeing their fellow angels while slitting the throats of the good angels that remain trapped in the debris.

Michael sees this and grows angry. "Blasphemy," he yells, taking up arms personally against Beelzebub. With his Sword of Fire, he smites the devil again and again until he knocks the staff from his enemy's hand. Beelzebub cowers, retreating back, scrambling across the ground like a frightened crab. He falls backwards into a hole, and Michael takes a position above him, raising The Sword. It begins to hum, static electricity building up on the surface of the weapon.

The deathblow is imminent, but several demons rush him, minions of Beelzebub mounting a rescue for their fallen leader. Michael swings at the new menace, only to have them disappear into vapors.

More demons approach. Michael grips The Sword tightly and swings with all his might, but as it connects they also vanish into smoke.

"What magic is this?"

Gabriel comes to his friend's side to help but the danger is past. They look down. The demons are gone and so is Beelzebub, vanished in smoke himself.

"The Fallen have the power of illusion at their command," says Michael.

"Their ability to present many faces," says Gabriel. "They use it to their advantage."

"Let's assess our position," says Michael.

They scan the battlefield. Many of his ranks are fighting phantoms and false enemies, wearing on their strength. In the foothills, Beelzebub's men have the high ground. On the mountain behind them a great horde is coming, eager to join them and led by Lucifer himself.

Michael raises the Sword above his head. It glows even brighter as he closes his eyes in prayer. "O Lord give me strength to fight this evil that descends from upon high and seeks to displace thee. Let me be thy weapon of goodness and deliver your justice."

The Sword begins to vibrate, charged by his words. It hums, a resonance that creates bright beams of light in all directions. The light illuminates the phantoms and the sound of The Sword shatters their fragile, transparent bodies. Only the truth remains. The fake images are gone, and The Sword stops glowing, the resonant hum continuing across a field free of false phantoms.

"Now," yells Haniel, one of Michael's seconds. "While you can see them. Attack."

Gabriel raises the horn to his lips and blows. The notes harmonize and add to the resonant sound. Divine instruments strike a chord from the back of God's lines and the Archangels are filled with a passion for victory. They form ranks and fighting units.

Michael's troops charge the Fallen Ones, their weapons raised, pikes and spears pointed forward seeking eager targets. Arrows fly in advance, and the eerie sound of the Sword of Fire continues to hang in the air as Michael prays to increase its power. Flaming arrows shoot across the sky glowing with death. Angels are struck, and on both sides victims fall to the ground, writhing and screaming in agony.

Urakabarameel reports to Beelzebub. "What can we do now? Our troops are routed, our tricks exposed."

"Attack with all your fury," orders Beelzebub. "We must hold them and give Lucifer the time he needs to win the ultimate victory."

"We can't beat them in a fair fight."

"Then don't fight fair," sneers Beelzebub. "You are pledged to the cause. We hold mystical weapons forged from falling stars, made white hot in the fires of Earth. They've been tested and they are unmatched in combat strength. Use them!"

"Aye," says Urakabarameel. "But Lucifer and his squad have the best weapons."

"Sharpen your points, then," says Beelzebub. "Hone them to a fine edge and prepare for engagement. Tell the men not to worry. We've got better tricks than the power of illusion to outwit these

Archangels. Just hold the lines. We only need a little time."

The thunder on the mountain is a reminder that Lucifer and his horde are on the way. For now, they are tiny figures in the distance moving like a scourge that spreads across the landscape. Raphael and Gabriel keep time and watch. "This is dangerous," says Raphael. "We could easily get drawn into their forces and surrounded."

"Halt the attack," yells Gabriel. He looks toward Michael for guidance but gets no response. The Archangel holds his Sword skyward in prayer.

Gabriel puts horn to lip and sounds the recall. Michael's army stops and regroups. Arrows continue to fly but it is relatively quiet on the battlefield. Over the silence, the thundering mob on the mountain slowly builds.

Gabriel stares into the distance. "Lucifer commits his forces. They are on their way to meet us." A flaming arrow whizzes by and he moves slightly to avoid it. It hits the ground nearby and fizzles.

"We should strike now, while their numbers are small," says Raphael standing next to him. "Make quick work of them while we order up our own reinforcements."

"You mean, use the Cherubim? What would you have them do here? Pray or intercede?"

"They have special power. God has ordered their release," says Raphael. "The holy beasts are reluctant to leave His side, but they will do what they are told. They could bring us victory."

"The Cherubim are strange angels, ferocious and different from us. But they should stay by God's side," says Gabriel. His eyes squint to see the growing figures on the mountain. "All this could be a diversion. After all, God is the real target, is He not?"

Seraqael joins them. One of the original seven Archangels to stand before God, he is also a field commander. "My angels are ready," he reports. "What is the delay? We should attack while they are weak and without reinforcements."

"That's what I said," cries Raphael.

"What do you say, Gabriel?" asks Seraqael. "Shall I give the order to advance?"

Gabriel looks at Michael who still holds The Sword skyward. He is focused and unmoved even as arrows land at his feet. His lips quiver in prayer and his words are muted. "Michael is supreme commander, Chief of the Presence. It is his word to give."

"Go ask him, then," says Seraqael.

"I will not disturb his meditation," says Gabriel.

Another arrow lands nearby. In the distance they hear cries as others not so lucky are struck. It is tense, the angels are nervous and ready. The thunderous mob on the mountain grows louder.

Beelzebub tries to fathom the sudden turn of events. "What are they waiting for," he says.

"Soldiers on the front send word that Michael is frozen," says Kola Zontor, the Destroyer. "One of our tainted arrows must have struck him. The enemy is without leadership. They don't know what to do."

The evil commander looks behind him at the hill.

"Then we'll give them something to do. Sound the advance."

Beelzebub's men shout and begin their charge.

37. Lambs for the Slaughter

Uriel, like Seraqael, is another of the original seven Archangels before God. He joins his fellow commanders. "What say you, Gabriel? We await orders. Or should we just stand and be slaughtered. What exactly is God's plan here?"

They look toward Michael. Gabriel approaches the praying angel, shielding his eyes from the brightness. "Michael," he whispers. "Palit, my brother. What is the word?"

He waits but there is no answer, only the resonant hum of The Sword and the silent prayers. Seconds pass like eternity. He turns away, returning to the band of generals.

"Well?" asks Uriel.

"He has no eyes," says Gabriel.

"What? What do you mean?"

"Look for yourself."

Michael prays. His eyes are two white sockets, his lips move with blurring speed, his words soft and inaudible. He grips The Sword but his hand is one with the hilt. The back of his wrist gleams silver. Prayers continue and the silver runs up his arm like liquid forming a gauntlet.

Beelzebub's forces draw closer, running headlong towards the enemy. Swords and spears extended, they aim at the hearts of the noble angels. Beelzebub uses his power to multiply their numbers a hundred fold. Overhead the flying brigades form again. The plains are alive with the rumble of feet and the flapping of wings.

"Michael," says Raphael nervously. "We're outnumbered. What shall we do?"

"We can at least defend ourselves," says Uriel. "Man the artillery. Get the holy weapons in place. You angels over there. Fight!"

Gabriel and Michael no longer have control. The mobs collide, a sea of bodies gripped in combat. Arrows flash overhead between bands of flying angels. They collide in mid flight, falling to the ground wrapped in struggle. Pikes and spears rain on them from both sides until they both lie still and silent in a death grip.

Blood drips on the plain from above. Angels cry out as their limbs are tested against the strength of forged metal. The sounds of suffering and the shouts of battle add to the thunderous noise of feet and wings and steel.

The illusions cast by Beelzebub spread confusion, and some angels fall forward in lost balance as they swing at phantoms. "What magic is this," remarks Uriel as he swipes at yet another phantom. "Michael's Sword no longer reveals the false demons."

Uriel swings again and this time his sword finds meat. There is a puff and instead of disappearing, the phantom changes into Sraosha, one of his own Captains. The loyal angel twists in death at the end of Uriel's sword.

"No!" yells the General but it is too late. Sraosha slides off the tip and drops in a bloody heap.

"What now?" asks Raphael. "There is no way to tell the difference between what is real and what is false. In confusion, we kill our own men."

Beelzebub summons more power around him. The ground shakes and the mountain shudders, pouring off rock and causing landslides that spread like talons to cover a corner of the battlefield. Forces on both sides are helplessly trapped beneath layers of rock and debris. Beelzebub nods in approval. "We took out more of them than us," he says. He shouts to his army. "Let their sacrifice not go unpunished." Spurred by this and the fury of their leader, the Fallen Ones charge again, attacking with new vigor.

The screams mount and the sweat of battle hang around all. Dust fills the air, creating a fog of war. Beelzebub's ground soldiers began to rake the air with grappling hooks, catching angels by the wing. Once snared, they pull them down and beat them unconscious while the hooks tear loose with dangling bits of damaged flesh.

"Michael," yells Gabriel. The leader does not respond. He hears only the sounds of his own whispered prayers. Swords clash close at hand as demons fight their way towards Michael.

"We must defend him," says Gabriel.

"What if one of them is my own men?" asks Raphael. "I don't want to kill them."

"Beelzebub forces us to make heinous choices," says Gabriel. "We must protect Michael while he is in a weakened state. We can't give up the fight." He slashes another phantom. As it turns to smoke, he cuts back with his sword and connects with another dark angel. As it slashes deep, the edge of the blade shimmers like a thousand spinning daggers. The demon's body separates above the stomach, landing on a pile that grows beside him.

A grappling hook catches Raphael, the barb drives deep into his chest pinning his sword arm. Spears and piles drive forward and he is met with pain on many points. He cries out again. "Michael!"

Michael twitches. He hears Raphael's call, listens to the shouts but does not move. Raphael falls forward, his body twists and lands beside one of the dead, dark angels. His eyes look off, empty of war, seeing only rest and peace. There is a mattress of bodies beneath him and as they settle, yet another body falls and Raphael is slowly concealed beneath a growing blanket of death.

Euronymous, one of Beelzebub's captains, steps on the pile of bodies and speaks to Azkeel at his side. "I'll take the horn blower," he says. "You get The Sword."

Azkeel nods. "I have a fraction of my two hundred now, but we can do it." His signals his men and together they begin fighting their way towards Michael.

"Don't fail me," shouts Euronymous. He raises his sword and rushes towards Gabriel, a hideous cry on his lips as he slices through the ranks.

Gabriel meets him head on. He lifts his own sword and blocks Euronymous, ducking as he lunges forward. The demon falls back, maneuvering low as he tries to jab upward at the angel. Gabriel whacks down on him, might and power behind every blow. Euronymous drops his sword under the relentless blows. Gabriel smiles and watches it clatter to the side. His eyes follow the fallen sword.

As he looks away, Euronymous takes an enchanted bodkin from beneath his cloak. With one swift stroke, he sweeps upward, gutting Gabriel. The noble angel's belly turns black, the flesh becomes liquid as the life pours out of him. In surprise he looks down at his belt, sees the dark blood dripping into the bell of the horn tied to his waist. He reaches for the instrument, as if to take it and play one last time, then falls forward.

Euronymous steps on the body, another stone on the path towards Michael.

The mighty Archangel witnesses this. His eyes return but his lips continue to whisper a prayer. He watches as his fellow angels are cut down like fall harvest. He squares his jaw, clenching his teeth. He holds The Sword out, gripping it tightly in his hand as he speaks to it.

But there is no hand. The fingers are fused, etched ridges, looking like the hilt once did. He cannot let go of it if he tried, The Sword and he are one, knitted together at the wrist in a single line of gleaming metal running up his arm. He nods in approval. "If ever we needed your power, my flaming friend, it is now," he says. "God trusted me with your power when he gave you to me. Now we join together to defeat this evil that threatens our homeland. I call upon you to reach inside yourself and once again bring forth your holy power to vanquish these foes. Light Heaven with your truth."

Light glows, and The Sword completes the joining of weapon and warrior. Fused to Michael's heart, they are ready to mete justice with power. The sword crackles, then gleams with the light of truth. It hums, drowning out the noise of battle. The fog of war clears and the fighting stops, everyone's attention drawn to the vibrating Sword of Fire. Michael is lost in the blinding display. There is only The Sword.

Rays shoot out from it as before. The loyal angels are revealed beneath the cloaks of illusion. Friend and foe are known to each other. The phantoms evaporate, leaving only the Fallen Ones, who now quake with fear. Under the light of truth, Beelzebub can cast no more illusions.

"Look! Their number is actually small," shouts one of Michael's angels. The reinforcements on the mountain become a scattered wreath of dots, their shouts an empty promise.

Michael lets out a roar unlike any heard before. All look toward him as he takes wing. Brandishing The Sword, he descends over the Fallen Ones like a hawk upon its prey. The Sword strikes once, then again and again. Sparks fly and the stricken ones retreat in terror and pain as their bodies twist and mutate beyond recognition. The Sword has found new power, the fire of transformation.

Michael strikes again. Skin turns red with blood, limbs warp, and wings deform into misshapen branches.

Beelzebub runs, and the mighty Archangel sets upon him with special vengeance. "Where do you seek to go, twisted one? There is no darkness that my Sword can not illuminate. No place for you to hide. Soon your outsides will match your insides and all will be able to see you for what you are."

Beelzebub knows this. He turns suddenly, his weapon charged with evil. He raises his spear, blocking Michael from striking him with The Sword. The sky cracks, and a nearby devil is struck with a stray lighting bolt that hisses from The Sword. Beelzebub turns the spear downward in a circle, managing to cut a gash on Michael's leg. The tip of the spear glows as he brings it up towards Michael's face. "You have met your match," he spits. "My spear has a longer reach than your sword."

Michael raises The Sword and blocks the tip again. Metal clangs and he retreats out of range, flying backward in a vortex of air. Beelzebub lunges, stabs with the spear, driving Michael further back.

Around them the battle escalates. Courage is found on both sides as they see their leaders fighting. New levels of fury erupt. Even the twisted and transformed ones emerge from beyond their pain to regroup and attack.

They strike again and again, but Michael and Beelzebub can find no weakness in each other's defenses. Neither tire of battle, and each blow seems to be stronger than the last. Fire blasts, white hot, but the metal of Beelzebub's magical weapon does not give against the power of The Sword of Fire. In every respect the weapons appear to be as equal as the opponents.

They fight with such tenacity that neither sees the tide of battle turn. Michael's forces have cornered most of Beelzebub's men in a canyon at the base of the mountain. They are driven towards the slaughter.

Surrender is immanent. Fighting stops as both sides watch their leaders clash. Almost as if the outcome of that single conflict would determine the fate of the war.

"If you throw down your spear," says Michael, "I will allow you and your men an orderly retreat to Heaven's gate."

"Retreat?" says Beelzebub, he jabs at The Sword, striking it in fun. Sparks fly. "Why would I retreat when our victory is at hand?" He taps The Sword again, a beguiling smile inviting Michael to play. "Ready for more?"

"Are you?" answers Michael. He raises The Sword and strikes angrily at Beelzebub, yet he senses something, a puzzle in his opponent's smile. "Where is your leader, that traitor Lucifer?" he asks.

"Yes," taunts Beelzebub. "Where is he? Where is Lucifer?"

"Let the coward show himself," says Michael, shouting to the mountains. "I am ready for him."

"You can't even defeat me," says Beelzebub. "To get to him you must first go through me."

Michael blocks another thrust, drawing his face near to Beelzebub. "By God's might," he whispers, close and personal. "You shall be vanquished."

The fight continues even as bands of Archangels begin to herd the Fallen Ones off in small groups towards the gates.

"God has ordered them cast out," says Rifion, an angelic guard. "It would be easier to defend Heaven with them outside the walls."

"Yes, says Halqim, guard of the north wind, assisting him. "But something worries me. With all the trickery revealed, there are so few of them here."

Rifion scans the battlefield. "The dead have not been counted yet. Perhaps that is where their numbers lie."

"Praise be," says Halqim. "We did it. We made short work of them."

"Perhaps," says Gradiel, the Might of God. He pokes at one of the Fallen with his spear, urging him on toward expulsion. "But where is Lucifer and the main body?"

Beelzebub hears the angels and sees his men being led from the battlefield in defeat. "I hope you're faring better," he prays to Lucifer. "With this action we have bought you time to move against God, but I believe we are about to see the price of that action."

Spinning in a dance, dizzy from battle, Beelzebub becomes weary. He half heartedly blocks a blow. The Sword comes close to his face and he stares into the glistening fabric of the steel blade. His eyes squint in the brightness of truth. The Sword hums gently to him, echoing the sound of his own weapon. As he stares into the glowing blade he sees something.

"What is that?" he mutters.

Michael does not answer. He is locked in tension with his enemy.

Beelzebub continues to mutter. "Is that what the face of Heaven looks like?" He squints. "Is that my soul?"

He is hypnotized. His eyes fill with tears. If asked, he would say from the bright light even though it is otherwise. His men are being led off to exile. His part in this drama is over, the rest is up to Lucifer. The mystical Sword of Fire stabs at his heart, not with metal but with its infinite power. In defeat Beelzebub lets his hands fall limp, clasping his weapon loosely and defensively.

Michael will not rest; he flaps his mighty wings three times, lifting himself over his enemy. Beelzebub falls sideways, surprised by the sudden move and the loss of tension.

Michael raises The Sword and strikes him through the head with it. Blood pours from the wound, covering Beelzebub's body and tuning his skin a bright red. Michael withdraws The Sword and horns grow out from the wound.

Beelzebub endures the change, reaches up to feel what has happened to him. His skin begins to erupt with scales, blisters, and open sores. Michael spins quickly in a circle and strikes him in the waist. His legs began to whither and twist and a hairy fur grows to cover him from the waist down. His feet melt into clove hooves, and his legs twist backwards into a strange position. Beelzebub drops his weapon and falls forward on his hands, sagging into submission.

Michael holds the glowing Sword over him, eager to strike and force new, more grotesque mutations on Beelzebub. The horned demon breathes hard. "I surrender," he says.

Michael levels The Sword at his throat. "Where is he?" he asks. "Where is Lucifer?"

"You are too late, warrior angel," he says. "Did you think he would not plan his move carefully?" he laughs, unable to resist the urge to gloat. "He always was your better, Michael, and now he proves it once again, for am I not the poorer of the prizes in this conflict?"

"You're prize enough for me, you misshapen carrion," Michael says. "Now move, and quickly. On to Heaven's gate."

Beelzebub rises slowly, stalling for time. He feigns weariness and exaggerates defeat, sagging along as slow as possible. He continues to taunt Michael. "While you busy yourself with me, who defends God?" he asks in a cynical voice. "Oh, yes, the Seraphim," he said. "But someone has to sing Lucifer's victory song. Why not them?"

"No talking," commands Michael. "Keep moving along."

"Funny how God was wounded. Did you know He could be wounded, Michael? Did you know God could bleed?"

"Shut up," Michael says forcefully.

"Lucifer has that blade even now, the one he used to wound God," he says. "He had it mounted on a staff more powerful than mine, a weapon more powerful than yours. A weapon powerful enough to use against God."

Michael brings the blade down hard along Beelzebub's back, and his spine erupts with protuberances, twisting him to hunch forward like an animal. Beelzebub scurries away, running like a scared ferret to escape further wrath from Michael. Inwardly he smiles knowing he has accomplished his goal. He gloats to himself, praising the cleverness of the master plan. "The confrontation between God and Lucifer is taking place now," he says. "Our forces will be in control soon. By the time we get to the gates, you may be the one expulsed, Michael."

The battle is over, the Plains of Heaven littered with carnage. The wounded are attended by angels of the Golden Legend, also called the Angels of Good Deeds. Some are healed in place, others must be loaded on litters and flown to a place of rest and treatment. The living follow Michael like a war mob. They sing victory songs and shout obscenities at the Fallen, behavior so unbecoming of angels. They move on, the noise becoming a fading din. The scent of death is everywhere, and the battlefield is as still as an empty glass of water.

My daughter and I have become sensitized and immune to the butchery. The taste of war lies bitter on our palates and we are in shock.

"Well, you have the answer to your question," I say. "I was wrong. Angels can die."

She starts to cry and I realize how thoughtless my words are. I take her hand and dry her tears. "Come on," I say. "I've had enough. Let's see if we can find a way out of my brother's memories."

38. My Affliction Explained

"Father, are you okay?" I hear the voice of my angel ask.

I am huddling on the ground, unaware that I have been in some kind of trance. My arms twitch. Recalling these events has taken its toll. It is the poison of my life sucked to the surface by exposure to my brother's memories. I have been in this state before. I find myself sweating and pawing at invisible enemies.

The family curse lives on through my brother's will. She has seen and witnessed everything I experience when I have an episode. She will soon know how I came to be afflicted. For now, she puts her arms around me, filling me with strength even as I continue to shudder uncontrollably.

"What's wrong?" she asks.

I retreat further inside myself, hoping to avoid unpleasantness.

"It's over," she says, stroking my head gently. "It's over, Daddy. There is no more war."

She is my little girl. He arm around me, I feel her love returning me to health.

"I don't see why it affects you the way it does," she says. "You were not there. Weren't you with Mother while the battle was raging?"

"Yes," I said. "I was with her, but I was infected by your Uncle. I carry the memories of his defeat, a little gift he gave me long ago."

"Infected?" she asks. "How can you become infected with bad memories?"

"They are nothing more than bad dreams, but they are vivid," I say. I am regaining my composure, my sanity returns in small chunks of logic. "Nightmares are in the realm of my brother. I do not know how he gained this power, but he cursed me with this weight."

"Is that what it's like for you?" she asks. "Do you relive the war like that?"

More chunks of logic seem to fall into place. I look around with a familiar strangeness to our surroundings. I should know this place. It is a cave of some sorts. "Do you know where we are?" I ask.

"I think we are back inside your memory stream." She points to a cleft in the rock. "That looks like the hole we crawled through after we came through the Firmament."

I recognize the fissure. The entrance to the Sacred Mountain.

"How do you feel?" she asks.

"Okay," I say. I turn and push myself up, staggering to my feet until I stand erect.

"There are angels around us," I say, noticing them for the first time.

"Yes," she says. "And it appears they are waking up."

She begins to fade, becoming etheric, a shade without substance. I call out to her but she has vanished.

39. Fear

Staggering to my feet I feel fear, for even an Archangel can know fear. I am becoming immersed in my own memories once again. The same fears that I felt originally are pressing in on me. As if waking from a dream, I realize that I am again a participant, unable to alter my history. And so I fall into my role as my personal drama unfolds.

"What's wrong?" asks Holly.

"I'm sorry," I say. "I'm a little disoriented. Where did you say we are?"

"Inside the Sacred Mountain," she says. She looks into my eyes and I have no secrets from her. "I sense your fear," she says.

"I have never been in such a confining space," I say. "In one sense it feels safe and secure in here, in another, like the walls are closing in around us."

"Like me, you are an angel of light," she says. "You are not used to being surrounded by stone and

darkness. You are not by nature a creature of the Earth. These are new experiences for you. Just relax and let them happen." She gently lowers me to the floor where I rest my back against a wall. I feel the Grail at my side, tied to my belt as it rests on the floor beside me.

Preparation is being made for the next part of our journey. This will be different than traversing the Firmament. I hear angels discussing options as they chart a complicated course based on their knowledge and memories. Soon, rest is over and I am driven to my feet as our journey continues.

The Light Within illuminates our surroundings. Dark shadows creep across the walls as we move, and there are hazards at every turn. The cavern, like the Firmament, robs us of all sense of direction. I have no idea of which way to turn, dependent on Holly for guidance. I wonder if this is what it is like to be abandoned by God, lost in a dark labyrinth that seems endless and oppressive.

Holly senses my apprehension. She makes conversation to help ease and distract me.

"You're an Archangel, aren't you?" she asks.

It is easy for her to capture my focus, for I am fascinated with her. Bold, adventurous, smart and sensitive, what's not to like? But I do not want to talk about myself, I want to know more about her. Somehow, words are stuck in my throat and I am unable to do anything but answer a simple "Yes."

"Then why aren't you up there in Heaven fighting the great battle?" she asks. "Isn't that what Archangels live for? To fight great battles in the name of God?"

"Some of us fight different battles."

"What's that supposed to mean?" she asks.

I want to tell her about the battle that rages within me, about the awful choices forced upon me, but I am ashamed. What would she think of me if I told her Lucifer is my brother? Would she still trust me?

When I don't answer, she puts her arm on my shoulder and says, "I'm sorry. I didn't mean to pry."

Now I am embarrassed. "I don't want to burden you."

"No burden" she says. "I'm an Angel of Mercy, and I thought I could lighten your load."

"It's not a load," I say.

"It is when you carry it all alone. Besides, I see your conflict. Do you think you keep it that well hidden? It's all over your face. In that stern look of fortitude you present." She reaches up and touches my face. I can feel oceans of tension float away in that caress.

"What do you mean?" I ask.

She laughs, not wanting to pursue that line of conversation. "I like you," she said. "You're not your typical Archangel, all arrogant and pompous, quick to raise a sword to solve any problem."

"The sword is not my source of strength," I say.

"Yes," she says. "I see that in you. Yet, like all Archangels, you struggle. Except this battle is not in Heaven, is it?" She looks deep in my eyes and I feel the nakedness of my soul under her gaze. "This struggle is within yourself."

My eyes widen, as if I have been caught. How does she know this? Are there other secrets she can sense?

"Oh, don't act so surprised. You've been moody and withdrawn ever since I first met you, but I have my suspicions that there's more to you than that." She sees the smile in my eyes, and adds, "I'm willing to stick around long enough to find out if I'm right. You know where to find me when you're ready to talk about it." She touches my cheek again. "I like having you around, Archangel." She turns away, concentrating on the path ahead of us.

My fear all but diminishes in that brief time spent with Holly.

Our path becomes hazardous again and we focus on the task at hand. Like the cliff descending through the Firmament, we move single file down a narrow trail along one wall of the cave. Beside us is a pit of darkness so black that it swallows the light from our hearts. A cold draft of air comes from that darkness, carrying with it a strange odor that I can not describe.

The trail is dangerous here. There is a noise up ahead. A misplaced step dislodges a rock and it tumbles, scraping the side of the wall on the way down until the sound is also swallowed in darkness.

An angel cries out in fear and loses their footing, falling into the pit.

"Flap your wings!" someone shouts.

Angels scramble into action, careful not to fall into the pit as well. Someone pulls out a stout rope and a rescue is underway. The ledge is narrow and blocked. On both sides we hold back giving the rescue team room to work. There are no outcroppings or stalagmites to secure the rope, the rock wall is smooth.

"Give me that," says Narsinha, a strong angel with sturdy Earth wings. "Secure this to my waist."

Once the rope is threaded and tied, he leaps from the precipice flying down over the edge. The rope plays out quickly and another rope is tied to the bitter end to extend it. The darkness swallows the angel, the light from within becoming a distant candle that is slowly extinguished. The second rope plays out and another is found and tied to it. It disappears into the darkness like Narshina.

The rope goes slack, a coil of it remaining on the ledge. Phanuel, an angel of hope, grabs the slack and pulls it taut.

"I feel a tug," he says with a smile. "Come on, now. Let's work together."

He and two other angels pull the rope while we take up the slack. The weight at the other end is heavy and limp. Tense moments pass. We peer into the darkness and see nothing.

"Pull, pull," orders Phanuel. He passes a knot in the line and shouts, "We are on the last rope."

A shape emerges out of the night below. There are shouts of joy when we see two angels on the rope, one held safely in the other's arms.

"That was close."

"It was horrible," says Gethel, the angel who had fallen. "There are strange vapors in this pit of darkness. I was overcome and would have been lost forever if you had not come for me."

The ropes are coiled and stored again and we compose our thoughts as we prepare to continue. As each of us look down into that void we know fear. It could easily have been any one of us.

We start again, moving slow and careful after Gethel's accident. The path soon leads away from that chamber and through a hole in the wall. Here we trade the fear of falling into the pit of darkness for the anxiety of solid, confining rock. The mountain rumbles, and the new danger is made all too clear. Dust shakes free of the walls as rocks and pebbles crack against the ground around us.

My claustrophobia has returned and Holly senses it. I talk to her as a form of relief. "I wonder if we could dig our way out of here if we were buried," I say.

"I doubt it," she says.

"Oh," I say. Not feeling any relief there.

"I'm sorry," she says. "Sometimes I'm too pragmatic. I just say whatever is on my mind."

"That's okay," I say. There is a pause and I push for conversation by asking. "What about you and your Neutral Angels? How long have you been around?"

"We have been gathering for some time. Many of us saw this fight coming," she says. "We took an oath of neutrality to represent the Middle Way. We love

and support God, we just can't fight His battles. Would you take up arms against your brother?"

Her question catches me by surprise. Does she know? "No," I say. "I love my brother."

"That was a rhetorical question. I meant that in the sense that we are all brothers, and sisters of course," she says. Her lips become an all knowing smile. "So, you have a brother?"

"Yes," I say. There is a moment of silence as she waits for more. "He's up there fighting. Tried to persuade me to fight with him but I didn't."

"So, you're neutral, too?"

"I guess so," I say.

"What do you mean, I guess so?" she chastens. "You prefer not to fight at all. You're not alone in that belief. There are a lot of us who are not polarized by the events in Heaven. We just want to continue in peace. We're the private citizens caught in a web of forces we can't control.

I nod in agreement. "What is the Middle Way?" I ask.

"It is neither good nor evil, it just is," she says.

"I don't understand," I say.

"There is nothing to understand. You just do it."

"Does this mean you worship neither God nor Lucifer?" I ask.

"It means neither," she says. "We adore God according to our nature. God is the source of our strength and we strive always to do good. We just try to make a conscious effort to keep our actions under control. We know that every action, especially below the Firmament, carries with it the capacity for both good and evil."

"I heard that from one of the angels at the gates of Heaven," I say. "What exactly does it mean?"

"All actions have consequences," she says.

"Yes, that is true," I say. "And I understand how each action can have both good and bad sides. If I save you from a falling stone I may die myself.

Good or bad? Who can judge in that case? Whose life holds more value: yours or mine?"

"But," she says, "We're both immortal."

"I'm not so sure of that anymore," I answer. "I saw God bleed and I didn't know it was possible. Until this time we thought war impossible, all we knew was peace. How do we know that death is not also possible?"

"No wonder you are so fearful on this journey," she says.

"I am more cautious than fearful," I say. I pat the Grail. "And I have work to do, it is motivation enough. But that does not change the fact that I would sacrifice all I had for you, even my own life." She stops and turns to stare at me. I look into her eyes, those mirrors to the soul, and I see a spark of meaning. My hand graces hers, and I speak. "Don't ask me why, but your life means more to me than mine does to myself. I would gladly sacrifice myself, just as I would sacrifice myself for the safety of this sacred cup I carry."

"How do you know that?" she asks.

"I just know it. That is the way I am," I say, sure of myself as I have ever been. "Perhaps it is the Archangel in me, come forth in a different way."

"Let's hope you never have to put that to test," she says. "Like I said, I like having you around, Archangel."

"But there is one thing more important than both of us," I say, gently placing my hand on the cup at my side. "You must promise that if something does happen to me, you will continue the mission to bring the Grail to safety."

"That's all well, but what if something happens to me?" she asks.

"Nothing can happen to you," I say. "You're the only one who knows where we are going. Without you we would all be running home."

She smiles. "You do me credit, but Irin the Watcher also knows the route. So does Vassago."

We take a few steps in silence when she asks. "Hey, what do I call you? What's your name?"

"I would tell you but you would not be able to pronounce it," I say.

"Oh, no?" she asks, thinking on that for a minute. "How do you introduce yourself to others?"

"I don't," I say.

"Okay, then. Hello. My name is Holly. What's your name?"

"I am one of the unpronounceable. I carry a personal name, a sound that is like a mantra within me. I have no translation for that. The closest thing to it might sound like Anglth-Mnu."

"Uhnglot-huem," she says.

"Close enough," I say.

"Inglith-Moo," she says.

"Better," I say. I stop walking and pull her aside. "Here, try this." I place her hand on my heart and she closes her eyes. I silently speak my name as only I can. Her lips move but no sound emerges.

She opens her eyes and nods, touches her fingers to my lips and smiles.

We continue walking. The way slopes downward and I feel water at my feet. More properly it is mud, and soon our feet begin to cake with dirt and debris. Movement becomes difficult. I want to lift myself out of the muck and fly away but there is rock overhead preventing it. I can think of no worse environment for an angel, a creature of the sky, than this hellhole.

The water becomes deeper and we pass a wall of seeping rock. In a few steps it seems to move from a trickle of mud at our feet to a small torrent. The water rushes us onward, and again I cling to the sacred relic lest I lose it.

A hundred steps further and the bottom drops. We are waist deep in water now, the relic at my hip in danger of washing away. I carefully tie it across my chest out of danger. The sound of rushing water fills our ears, and our feet struggle to find purchase. The water is cold and penetrating, chilling body and slowing reactions. Wings are useless and wet and they drag against the moving water. The Light from Within flickers and the darkness around us resumes with a new vengeance.

The small passageway goes on and on, alternating between narrow and wide. We scrape against rock, glancing against the sides as the current pushes us forward. There are surges and we are buffeted about, cut by sharp objects.

There is another drop and the current moves faster, fed by another stream of water. In one large push, we are thrust down a long chute moving ever faster. At the mercy of the water the force is relentless. Wings threaten to snap, limbs to break. We bump into each other. I bob to the surface, inches away from the rock ceiling, barely enough room to open my mouth and catch a breath. I turn to face forward, my feet bracing for impact. A stalagmite hangs ahead of me and I duck below the surface and to the side. The rock walls are unforgiving and damaging. There are feathers floating around me, pieces of rope and supplies that have come loose. I place my hands firmly on the Grail, curling around it to protect it from loss or impact.

The pace of the water quickens. I surface for one more breath before I plunge into a vortex of water that draws me downward into the dark depths below me. I try to fight it but it pulls me deeper. Helpless, I abandon my struggle and brace myself for whatever lies ahead.

There is a rush and my ears pop. I spin in the maelstrom of water until it narrows around me. With *a mighty burst it pushes me through a tight fissure, ejecting me into an underground lake.*

A hand grabs my forearm. "Are you all right?" asks Holly.

My breath is heavy, as if each gasp were that of someone drowning.

"Can you stand up?" asks Holly. "It's not very deep." She tugs at my arm and I right myself. There is water to my waist and my feet press against soft sand.

"I can't see you," I say.

"That's because of the steam," she says. "This chamber is filled with warm, white clouds. The Light from Within is useless."

She is right. The Light from Within reflects back at us, illuminating the surrounding clouds of steam with white, leaving us blinded by our own light. It is the antithesis of darkness yet it has the same effect. Movement is difficult, and we can not see ahead of us any longer.

"We can't stay here. Let's get going," she says. She disappears in the mists.

"Wait," I say. "I can't see you." I wade and splash at the water like a panicked child.

The mist speaks back. "Then follow my voice."

I take small steps, groping the fog with unsure hands. I feel something soft and tangible.

"You found me," she says. Once again I sense love and protectiveness from her, stirring my own feelings to be closer to her and learn more about her.

She has within her some innate compass that can pierce the fog. Some of us link hands in a chain so we don't wander from each other. We are a band of stragglers following the voice of an angel.

Holly starts to sing. The melody has a soothing effect as it echoes off the ceiling of the chamber. The sound is amplified and the rock returns it to us with strength and power. It acts as a beacon to her voice and we follow it like a lifeline. The gentle splash of water adds to the overall calm that descends upon us as we make our way across the shallow lake. The warm, steamy mist, though not too uncomfortable, surrounds us with a blanket of white.

The chamber begins to constrict into a tunnel again, although much larger than before. Temperatures change. We wade through that tunnel, our lower half immersed in cold water, our upper half surrounded by boiling steam. This new torture has an interesting consequence, for whenever two opposites are combined, the effects seem greater. In this instance, the cold is more frigid and the heat more searing. The way becomes forced and labored now and I don't know how long we can endure this union of extremes.

Above all we continue to hear Holly sing. It helps distract our minds from the pain around us, focusing our strength inside. This is the true power of prayer and adoration, and without this strength and guidance many of us would become lost in that underground world forever.

We move slowly onward. The chamber narrows again, constricting even more. My wings scrape against the ceiling. We no longer hold hands, it is easier to move freely in the small area and no one can get lost.

The bottom drops. We sink deeper into a stream of cold water with only our shoulders and heads remaining above. I hold the cup up high, plodding along with my feet while I try to balance myself with wet wings. The echo of Holly's voice is swallowed in the tight quarters and it does not carry the same effect. She stops singing as we continue single file down the passage. With all my might I hold tightly to the cup, protecting the blood of God within it from being washed away in the current. My arms soon ache and long for release from this new torment.

Helpless to change the past, a participant in my own history, I endure these tortures again. At my weakest, the danger escalates to a new level of threat. The tunnel narrows once again. The current picks up speed and the level of water rises. My head dips below the surface. I hold my breath, the gift of life given by God. My lungs burst with agony and I gasp, waiting for another opportunity to breathe. I strain to keep from drawing my next breath, ready to lose consciousness.

I sense an air pocket and I bob to the surface and gasp. My legs strain to stay in position. I lift my head above the water and try to take a full breath but I am struck from behind by another angel. We tumble forward, scraping against rock, my wings taking the brunt of what is meant for my head. I curl into a ball, the chalice gripped tightly in my hands at the center for protection. The sound of rushing water fills my ears.

I strike against something and come unraveled. No longer a ball, I am buffeted like a rag against the stone. Pain stabs at me, cuts and scrapes, torn feathers, and abrasions. I want to breathe, to pull in air and feed my body with relief. I become dizzy turned upside down by the force of the water yet I somehow manage to hold on to the Grail.

It must be true that God does not burden us with more than we can handle, for I am at my end.

The tunnel narrows one last time. I hold my hands above, the chalice bumping against the ceiling, the rocks and outcroppings trying to wrest it from my hands. I pull it to my chest trying to protect it when suddenly I fall through a hole into a larger cavern.

I hit the floor with a thud, my hands extend with the cup resting upright before me. The cloth around it is damp but the precious object inside is dry and intact. The plate that covers the chalice is still fixed tightly over it, and I know the blood of God rests safe inside.

A waterfall has deposited me on a small, relatively dry shelf. The water turns and drains in a different direction. I pull myself out of the shallow stream and onto the beach. As I lay there, my fellow angels fall one by one around me, thrust from a hole about thirty feet above. The sound of the water is both deafening and soothing as it echoes off the cavern walls. Above the waterfall steam emerges from the hole, spiraling upward into an engulfing blackness, hissing and adding another level of noise to the ambient sounds.

I stand up, carefully holding the cup while I study my surroundings. We are in a huge room, a high ceiling cave, filled with stalagmites and stalactites. The floor is uneven, bending every which way. Strange rock formations cling to the walls, shingles and colored patches of lumpy clay, luminous projections and veins of glittering ore. The source of the steam is visible, a fissure along one wall that contains glowing rock. A horrible stench fills the air around us.

"Brimstone," says one of my companions. "It is the smell of sulfurous rock, ignited by the fires that live beneath the Earth,"

"I have not smelled it before," I say.

"It is common in areas of volcanic activity," he explains. "It is poisonous, and we should leave quickly lest it infect us with its putrid flavorings."

"The taste has a way of lingering," says Holly. "The last time I passed this way and breathed these vapors they stayed with me all the way back to Heaven."

We regroup and the warmth returns to our bodies, along with the Light from Within. It gradually illuminates the space around us. We help our fellow angels to their feet, reestablishing their balance and their dignity. We all wear soiled robes, hardly angelic, full of bruises and missing feathers but nonetheless intact. The stream carried mud and dirt, and many of us had scraped ourselves against the walls. Yes, angels can feel pain, and even fatigue and loneliness. We long to cleanse ourselves in the pure waters of Heaven, though we are far from home.

It is eerie. Shadows play against the walls, flickering as if in candlelight. I cannot see beyond them, and they present a new challenge. The room is a maze of confusing shapes between the rock spires. The waterfall continues to crash behind us, beating the rocks with a deafening noise that echoes through the cave. The river at its base adds to the cacophony as it runs along one wall a short distance then disappears into a sump in the floor.

"I'm lost," I say. "And there is no exit to this room."

"We can go back the way we came," says Holly.

The color drains from my face.

She laughs. "No," she says. "We won't be going that way."

"Is this the final resting place of the Grail?" I ask. "It seems far enough and hidden from eyes."

But it is not. I know the answer even as my lips ask the question. Again I find myself the unwilling participant in my past. I want to shout to my companions, share what I know but that is not possible. For as we idly chat anticipating the next phase of our journey, we are being observed. Behind each pillar and lurking in each shadow is an enemy. The Fallen Ones discovered this place before us, using it as an assembly point for the unfortunate souls who were already cast out. We have stumbled into their kingdom of darkness, and no matter which direction we choose, there will be inescapable danger.

Even as the battle takes place on the Plains of Heaven above, coordinated with the confrontation between God and Lucifer, there will be a third battle beneath the Earth, and despite an oath of neutrality, the angels of the Middle Way will have no choice but to fight in their own defense.

40.   The Room of No Exit

I listen carefully, trying to discern the footsteps of the Fallen, but the noise of the waterfall drowns out any hope of that. For unknown reasons, the light from within is slowly fading. I peer into the darkness and see nothing but phantoms created by my mind, imagined fears that refuse to go away.

"What do we do now Father?" asks my daughter.

I turn around, my brain in a fog. "What are you doing here?" I ask. "Don't you know the danger you're in? Get out of here. Now!"

"It's okay," she says calmly. "It's just a memory. Your memory."

I look around. I don't remember it like this. Dark shapes play across the cavern walls. Demons eye us from every shadow. The smell of brimstone is overpowering.

"This is not my memory," I say. I look around for Holly and my friends but there is only my daughter and I. "Where have they gone?" I ask. "Did they leave without me?" I touch my belt and the Grail is missing. I panic.

She tries to help, places her hand on my arm. "It's okay," she says. "We're in a memory."

There is a growl from behind a nearby rock. I turn and stare into the darkness again. Another growl. Her hand leaves my arm and she moves behind me. There is movement ahead of us, I can feel it.

"You should listen to her," says a voice from out of the dark. It draws near. The shadow gives way to the face of Lucifer. He smiles. "Memories can be powerful, can't they, brother?"

I frown. "This is no memory."

"You're right," he says. "It's a dream. But does that make it any less real?"

"A dream?" she says.

"Yes," says Lucifer, turning toward her. "You see, I have some power over the dream world. Always have."

"How did we get out of my memory?" I ask.

He turns to me. "Memories are so like dreams," he says. "Personal and open to interpretation. When we recall them, they are not always clear and exact."

"Mine are," I say. "I like my memories. Please return us there."

He turns to her, draws a deep breath. Kindly old Uncle Lucifer is back, his disarming smile accompanying his easy demeanor. "How about you, dear? You finished with me?"

She smiles coyly.

"I thought not," he says. "You still have questions, don't you? Let me see if I can guess a few. What happened when I confronted God? What about the fate of Michael and his army of Archangels? What about your dear Uncle Lucifer and his humble story? You hunger to know the rest, don't you?" He produces the apple again. "Am I right?" He offers it to her. "Are you hungry?"

She takes the apple from him but does not eat of it. "And if I am? Will this satisfy my hunger?"

"I don't know," he says. "How hungry are you?"

She takes a bite and offers it to me.

I have no choice but to join her. I take the fruit of the Tree of Knowledge, somehow altered to his own whim, and with one bite, I am back in his game.

41 Satan Begins Again

The dream fades, replaced by another. We are no longer in a dark cave but in the brightness of Heaven. We walk behind my brother, part of his entourage headed for the celestial throne of God. We are unwilling followers. I am just as much a witness to my brother's memories as I am to my own. I know the tale from discussions with other angels, witnesses to Lucifer's actions, but it seems so real now.

The hiss and cries of the Cherubim remind me that we are cast as enemies in Lucifer's drama. These beings are more creature than angel, almost an angelic reflection of the Fallen Ones. They are huge with wings and animal faces, some with bodies of bulls or sphinxes. They are the holy beasts with a thousand eyes and they are terrifying as their rage and anger is directed toward us.

Lucifer walks confidently into God's presence. He waves his spear before the Cherubim, threatening them with violence. It glows green and even though they retreat from it, they do not stop their infernal wails and cries.

"I come in peace," says Lucifer, even though his recent actions betray otherwise. "But if you bother me I'll take you to task." He waves the spear, blinding a thousand eyes with its green glow. "My business is with God and not you."

"God's business is our business," says a lion-bull beside him, six eyes trained on me. "You don't belong here. You have been ordered cast out."

Lucifer stops and raises his hand. Our procession halts as he removes his cloak and lays down his spear. One of his men rushes forward, picks them up, and carries them away. "See how I am unarmed?" he says, opening his hands and lowering his head in supplication.

"So you *can* bow," says one of the Seraphim, his words roaring with power. His four faces peer down at us while his six wings beat nervously at his back. The Cherubim back away, allowing the Seraphim to take charge. We are close to God now, surrounded by these holy angels, the inner ring of His divine hierarchy. They are the serpent angels of love, light, and fire and the last guard we must pass through before audience with the Creator.

"I have no problem bowing," says Lucifer, lowering himself again. "I live to serve God." He smiles, letting the grin turn to a frown as he spits on the ground. "It is Man I detest."

God speaks. We hear Him from behind a crowd of angels but do not see Him directly. "How can you detest Man, Lucifer. We have made him in Our image," He says. "He is a divine being and is as worthy of your servitude as I am."

"No!" says Lucifer. "He is not above the angels." He speaks to the assembled angels, seeking a supporter among them. "We were here first," he says.

"God has decreed it," says Barakiel, ruler of the order of Seraphim. "It matters not who came first. Do you place one set of angels above another just because they were the first born of God?"

"A noble idea," suggests Lucifer, his smile returning.

"Lucifer, you are still my favorite," says God. "Why do you seek to displease me?" The Cherubim and Seraphim part, allowing the antagonists to face each other as they talk.

"My Lord," he begins, taking another step forward. Angels quickly put themselves between him and

God. Lucifer stops his advance. "I love You, O Lord. And You say You love me. Why is it that You displease me?" he asks. "Why do You waste Your time with Man?"

"Because, though I have created the Angels to live on high, some are flawed," replies God

"Flawed!" shouts Lucifer in amazement. He is sure these words will gain followers from the audience. "We are flawed?" he asks the crowd.

"Yes, you are flawed," repeats God. "But I still love you," He says. "You are my Star of the Morning."

"How can we be flawed?" asks Lucifer. "Are we not made in Your image as well, O Lord?"

Never before have I heard my brother's words so sincere. There is love in every breath, and though I do not side with him, my heart bleeds for his cause as I feel his pain.

But there is also pain in God's heart.

"Not quite, My son," He says. "True, you are made in My image, and I love you, but you are flawed."

This angers Lucifer, and God can see it in his eyes.

"Look at yourself," says God. "I see the conflict in you. We all do."

"What conflict?"

"Love and hate. They fight within you even as you fight Me outwardly."

"Are you saying I represent hate and you represent love?" asks Lucifer.

"You are both," says God. "And neither."

"What does that mean?" asks Lucifer. "You speak in riddles."

"I speak in truth," says God. "Again I ask, why do you oppose Me?"

"I don't oppose You," says Lucifer. "I oppose Man."

"But you disobey me," says God. "You disobey Me and still I love you. All I ask is that you serve Man as you would serve Me."

The conflict boils inside Lucifer, his face dances with emotion. Torn between choices, he grapples with himself, his face twists with each thought. In a sudden move of surprise, he drops to his knees, perhaps sensing the horns of his dilemma for the first time. "I want to serve You, O Lord. Please let me serve You."

"To serve Me is to serve My will. And My will is for you to serve Man," says God firmly.

"Please, God," he says, beginning to sob. "Please!"

My heart breaks. We bear witness as Lucifer crumbles. He loves God more than anything. Anyone could tell, the agony on his face is plain. His body twitches as he cries, as if every muscle within him is in pain and conflict. Never has there been such a display of agony and love. "Please, God. Ask anything of me. Anything but that."

"It is My will," God says after a long pause. "My will."

"Please," cries Lucifer. "I love You. You are wrong, don't You see it? Listen to me. I still love You."

"My will, not thine be done," says God.

"But I love You," says Lucifer, almost pleading now. His eyes are buried in his hands, his face hidden from view.

Great is the conflict within my brother, for in a moment of desperation, he loses all control of himself. I can not say if it is love or if it is pain that motivates him. I do not judge his action and I refrain from calling it evil. These things address the very nature of love. Perhaps it is just another act, which has both good and bad consequences. Whatever it is, whatever motivation, Lucifer rises. When he takes his hands away there are tearstains on his face.

It is also a signal, for at that moment, Lucifer spreads his hand to the side. Dumah, the angel of silence and death, steps forward from behind me and places the spear in Lucifer's hand. He hurls it forward with all his might, aimed right at the very heart of God.

God does not flinch. Angels move quickly, placing themselves before God in an effort to protect Him. It is too late, the spear floats past them, driven with the might of Lucifer behind it, twisted sinew in conflict, a driving force that can not be denied expression. The spear moves closer to God's heart. The Creator freezes, waiting for the inevitable. As the spear draws near all eyes turn, some in pain, some in praise, some in utter disbelief.

Lucifer's men spring into action, attacking now with all their strength. Spears and arrows fly as swords and shields are lifted. The Seraphim roar, gruesome shouts that quiver deep inside me. I duck as a talon sweeps past my cheek. One of them reaches for my daughter, ready to shred her into confetti, a lion with human hands and the body of a bear. Dumah pulls a rag out of his pocket. It is a tattered cloak that he throws across my daughter's shoulders. The talons pass through her as if she were invisible.

I nod my thanks to Dumah. He reaches inside a small shoulder bag at his hip and pulls out a shield. It is thrice the size of the bag and my eyes open in wonder. I catch it and fasten it to my forearm just in time to receive a sword also pulled from the bag.

Archangels are trained in weapons. I studied under Azazel, one of the best. I grasp the sword but it is heavy in my hand. My will lies elsewhere and I would sooner wound myself than strike one of God's holy angels. The Cherubim think otherwise and I raise my shield just in time to deflect a deadly row of teeth aimed at my neck.

With Lucifer's spear less than an inch from His chest, God slows time. That is the only way I can explain it. The spear hangs in mid flight pointing at its target. God's bare chest is visible through the front of His robes. The spear moves closer as time slows even more until everything stops completely. To the right of God are a Seraphim and a Fallen Angel locked in combat. One holds a sword at the other's throat while the other tears at the opponent with sharp claws. Beside them are two Cherubim in mid air, twisting in agony as one is skewered by a spear and the other is about to be. Close by, another of God's angels lay prone on the ground pinned at the neck by the foot of one of Lucifer's men. Everywhere are signs of combat, frozen in a silent deathscape of statues.

God steps out from behind the spear and walks among the twisted figures studying the faces sculpted by His own hand. They are taut with agony and hatred. Brother fights brother and the division between His holy angels threaten all He has created. It is the collapse of His kingdom.

In every direction there is destruction. Smoke rises from the distant plains, once green and fertile, now dark and broken. Beneath His feet the foundation is weakening, unable to support the weight of troubles that plague Heaven. The air itself is thick with emotion weighing heavy on the spirit.

He walks over to Lucifer. "Is this what you want?" he asks. Lucifer does not move. "Don't stand there like a statue," says God. "I know you are aware of everything right now."

Lucifer trembles and comes to life. "I'm sorry, My Lord," he says. "I fear Your wrath."

"As you should," says God. "What do you hope to gain by all this, Lucifer?"

"My own kingdom and with it my own destiny," he replies.

"An honest answer," says God. "But was this the way to go about it? Turning brother against brother? And now you turn against Me!"

The tearstains deepen. Lucifer looks around at the frozen images. "I'm sorry," says Lucifer. "I love You."

"This is the price of your kingdom. Do you see the horror of your deeds?"

He hides his face again. "Yes." Sobs. "I let it go too far."

At this moment his fall from grace is complete.

"Tell me Lucifer, what will you make of Heaven?" asks God.

"I would make it a paradise," he replies.

"Is it not a paradise already?" asks God.

"Yes, it is, O Lord. Truly it is," says Lucifer. "But it is Your definition of paradise and not mine. I would not include Man in any of my plans."

"And why is that?" asks God.

"I told You, Man is flawed."

"And so are the angels," replies God, drawing his attention to the frozen figures around them. "But Man will find a place in Heaven one day, I grant you that."

"Man will disappoint you," says Lucifer. "I will grant You that."

God shrugs. "Why do this, my son?" he asks. "Is it ego? Is it rivalry and jealousy over your brothers? Is it fear that I will ignore you? Have I taken more of an interest in Man than is comfortable for you?"

"You made me, Lord," Lucifer replies. "You know the answer to that."

"Yes, but do you know?" God asks. He peers deep into Lucifer's eyes. "I can see your innermost thoughts, even the ones you keep hidden from yourself. Do you know why you did it?"

God sees the soul of His creation. Lucifer's eyes go white and his gaze is turned inward.

What it is like to have your soul laid bare, to see yourself without reservation, the hidden and the known, all visible at once. Would you understand the architecture of the self enough to learn from this? Or would you go mad knowing there were things you could not change despite your beliefs, despite your best efforts. Flaws by design, broken pieces meant to interact in some meaningful way that only the Creator understands.

Lucifer is not alone in his knowledge. The eyes of God see all, a diamond appraiser, gently rotating my brother's soul and studying the light as it reflects on the many facets of his being. What is it like to have the eyes of God upon such things? What did The Master Appraiser see inside my brother?

Lucifer breaks the silence. "What will become of me?" he says, uncomfortable, desperately wanting to change the subject. He will say anything to avert God's eye.

"You prove me correct. I know that the angels are flawed, that is why I gave them Grace. But I also withheld Grace from some of them, and that compounded the flaw. You are flawed and you have fallen from grace Lucifer. The Kingdom of Heaven is no longer open for you and your followers."

"I thought as much," says Lucifer. "Is it better to rule or to serve?"

"Both have their value," says God. "And their cost. I have ordered you cast out, and so it shall be."

"Man is also flawed," says Lucifer again. "You are blind to that. If angels are flawed, does it not follow that all Your creations are flawed? What kind of creator are You?"

God speaks kindly to my brother. "I made you imperfect. How else could you strive for perfection?

You keep looking for flaws in Man and not within yourself." He is sad. "What I wanted for you was so different than what you chose."

He turns his back on Lucifer and walks slowly toward his throne. God sits down wearily, the exact place as before. He carefully positions his chest in front of the spear, his robes open, lying on his unwounded side.

Lucifer nods, moves back to where he had been standing.

"Man will fall too," says Lucifer.

"Will you see to that?" asks God.

"I'll make it my mission," says Lucifer.

God nods gravely at him. The tip of the spear touches His skin and time begins to move again.

The skewered Cherubim fall to the ground, a spear thrust through them. The seraphim and the Fallen One locked in combat come to life. There is a gash at one's throat while the other starts to bleed from talon inflicted wounds. An angel pinned to the floor gags with choking sounds. Others around them thrash about in combat. Lucifer spins in confusion watching the melee unfold in all directions.

The spear dimples against God's skin. He reaches up and takes it in His hand before it can penetrate. He breaks it in half and casts it aside. "Lucifer, I have had enough. You want my kingdom? Go to hell!"

The base of Heaven around God opens up and spreads. Loyal angels hover safely in mid air, while the ground under us opens. I feel a pang of fear looking down into the abyss, the Firmament far below, as distant as a far-flung ocean. I instinctively flap my wings but they do not work. None of them do. We hang there, unknown forces holding us still, the void below waiting to swallow us.

Lucifer and his band begin to fall. First his men. They drop like stones into a deep pool of water, creating waves and splashing coarse matter as they hit the surface of the Firmament. Down further they go, falling through the murky depths toward Earth. They are wrapped in the gooey mass that separates Heaven from Earth, thrashing as if they had been dropped into a pool of acid. Forces pull at them as they sink, their bodies twisting into new shapes as they squirm in agony to escape their hideous transformations.

The Creator opens his hands and a vortex forms between them. Images take shape, projections of events elsewhere, a way of showing Lucifer that His word is final. We gaze into the vortex and see the gates of Heaven where Beelzebub and his defeated army are thrown mercilessly over the precipice. They fall at different speeds and trajectories. Some strike the Earth with such fury that they tear new canyons, crack open volcanoes, and create deserts. Others settle gently, like leaves floating in a breeze. Some land in the midst of the Neutral Angels guarding the retreat on top of the Sacred Mountain.

On the Plains of Heaven, mounds of dirt rumble. Bodies buried beneath the debris of a landslides rise up, the dirt falling from their robes as they stand in Heaven's light. Gabriel stirs, no longer lifeless, his body healed by the power of God's love. He raises his horn to his lips and blows triumphant.

Everywhere, life is restored where there once was death. Angels are healed and bathed in the light. The Seraphim begin to chant once again, intoning the sacred "Holy, holy, holy."

The Cherubim change, glorious mutations that transform them from holy beasts to innocent children. Gone are the hundred eyed monsters, replaced with smiling cherubs that flutter gently at God's side.

The Fallen are not so lucky. They become the unholy beasts, monsters and liars, deceivers exiled to a land of fire.

Lucifer begins to fall, slowly at first, then with increasing speed, until Heaven becomes a distant memory in the former Archangel's eye. He curses God as he falls, his wrath sworn in a line of obscenities. His voice cracks the sky like lightning, his words echo like thunder. He strikes the Firmament and his voice is muffled beneath layers of coarse matter.

God turns his attention back to his kingdom and the task of rebuilding Heaven.

My daughter and I hover over the opening, my brother and his entourage gone from our presence. I look down from dizzying heights, into an abyss that just swallowed my brother. We hang there, our robes flapping in the breeze, waiting for whatever fate there is for us.

The wait is not long. We too begin to fall. Wings are useless and my skin begins to burn as we accelerate. The Firmament rushes up at us like a platter.

"Protect yourself. Curl into a ball like me," I yell to her as I demonstrate. We strike the Firmament with unprecedented force. Our speed increases as we hurtle downward, plunging through thick, coarse matter that etches our skin with pain.

It burns, and I wonder if it is the transformation process. We were part of Lucifer's entourage. Has my brother somehow tricked me into this fate?

I feel myself tearing apart, a meteor falling to Earth. My daughter has passed out. Her eyes are closed and she tumbles like a rag doll. I reach out. There is nothing I can do to help her. In a cloak of agony, I black out.

42 Dream within a Dream

"Are you okay?" asks Holly.

I shake my head. "What happened?"

"I'm not sure," she says. "You were lying quiet on the floor, your eyes closed, gently breathing."

"I was asleep," I say.

She looks at me funny.

"Asleep," I say, but she has no concept of it. I point down to my daughter, lying peacefully asleep on the floor beside me. "See?"

Holly looks down. "I see nothing."

I turn and she is gone, only a cavern floor remains. Where did she go? There is a tug at my mind, a tightness, as if I were donning a mask. That feeling is back, and once again I am powerless over my actions.

I have awoken from my brother's dream into my memories, again an unwitting participant in my own history.

43 The Grail Mission Continues

"Looks like everyone is rested enough," says Holly. "We'd better get moving."

"Our group stands slowly, the pain of our passage not soon forgotten. Our clothes are tattered and there is dirt on our faces. The waterfall is a reminder of where we came from, deafening all thoughts around us. Irin, the Watcher, points the way forward, a path between two rock pillars that leads to a dark hole across the cave.

And so we begin again. I secure the Grail to my belt and feel its familiar comfort. Others gather up ropes and supplies, hoisting them on their backs or tying them to their waists. The thunder of the waterfall pales as we wearily trod onward. We barely take a hundred steps when Holly senses something. She holds her hand up and halts our advance. "What's that noise?" she asks.

"I hear it too," I say.

The cavern springs to life about us. From around each pillar and rock emerges a twisted shape. They pop up everywhere, stepping from behind stalagmites and from inside crevasses and out of deep shadows cast across the floor of the cave.

"Fallen Angels," I whisper, my breath forced and harsh. I pivot to find our band completely surrounded by demons of all sorts, the twisted remnants of the first outcasts. They brandish swords and staffs and threaten us with talons and fists and fangs.

"Yes," shouts one of them, coming forward as he growls like an animal. "Fallen Angels."

We are hopelessly outnumbered. Despite my fear, I retain my calm and step forward. "First to arrive?" I ask.

"Yes," says the leader. "And this is our land now. Get back to Heaven where you belong." His voice is familiar but I do not recognize the distorted shape before me.

"We are Neutral Angels," I say. "We have no squabble with you. Let us pass."

This is met with a tittering of laughter. I can hear ragged comments.

"Let's just kill them now," says one.

"I would enjoy eating them alive," says another.

"God help you now, my little angels," taunts a third.

Holly comes forward and stands beside me. "I'm the leader of this expedition. I'm responsible for these angels."

"Then maybe we should eat you first."

"Hold your words," I say. "We mean you no harm."

A three horned demon steps forward. "What if we mean to harm you?"

I tire of diplomacy. It does not seem to work on these creatures. They have a taste for violence. "I'm not sure you want to do that," I say, posturing. Instinctively my wings fan out, making me appear larger. My eyes narrow, piercing him with an Archangel's stare.

Holly speaks. "We are just passing through. We don't intend to settle here."

"Why not," one of them hisses. "Something wrong with our home?"

"You just need to get used to the place," says another, looking around the cavern. "All this darkness grows on you."

There is a shout from someone in the shadows behind them. "Hold them! Lucifer would love some prisoners to torment. He might even reward us." There are nods and agreements from the mob.

I ready myself, my duty to protect the Grail. I balance this with the safety of those around me. It is time to test my resolve, an oath I made only a short time ago to this sweet Angel of Mercy. I told her I would gladly sacrifice all I have for the safety of her and her companions. The time of testing has arrived.

I take a step closer and the demons react. Some lean forward, but most step back. Though I stare resolutely forward, my vision scans the periphery, evaluating options and considering courses of action.

From out of the shadows steps the leader of this group. The smart ones always lie in the shadows, *letting the rank and file test the enemy while they observe and calculate. "You!" he says, his voice fierce and commanding. He comes towards me for a close inspection. "I recognize you," he says, studying my features.*

I study him back, seeing in his eyes some faint resemblance to someone I once knew. He is not as I remember him. This creature is tormented; the left side of his body is larger than the right, causing him to walk with a limp. His legs are bent back and triple jointed, more livestock than angel. He is red all over, the color of fresh blood glistening from an open wound. He has an elongated, rodent-like face bearing pointed yellow teeth that are bared in a wicked smile. He drools as he talks. "Yes, I recognize you," he says. "You are Lucifer's brother."

Holly gasps. My fellow angels are astonished. Even some of the Fallen Ones stand back in shock.

"Yes," I say. "I am his brother."

"Then he is one of us," shouts a Fallen Ones.

"No," I answer. "I took no sides in this conflict."

"We are Neutral Angels," says Holly, adding her voice to mine.

"What does that mean?" asks the leader.

"We do not agree with my brother," I say. "And neither do we agree with Michael. We choose not to participate in the conflict. War does nothing to bolster the tranquility of Heaven."

"An excuse," one of them accuses. The demons are aroused, murmuring among themselves and plotting my fate and the fate of my band.

"Yes," I shout over them. "Perhaps it is an excuse. I don't know. I made no decision, and I still refuse to take sides."

"Then what are you doing here? Spying?" asks the leader.

"No," says Holly. "We are on a mission."

"A mission from God?" jeers one of the demons behind me. He titters and I glance around, noting that we are still surrounded.

"No," I say, I turn and face the titter. "It is our own mission, a mission undertaken by the Neutral Angels. Now I ask you again to please let us pass."

"Or what?" says the leader. "Will you then attack us with your fierce neutrality?"

I look at him again, seeing the features of a friend and not an enemy. His voice rings in my heart and I recognize one of my brother's comrades. I remember him as a good angel, one with whom I shared many a warm conversation, one I called friend, no, one I still call friend.

Perhaps he was confused by my brother's words. Where is his smile now? I wonder if he had a chance to do it over again, would he choose a different path? There is sadness in his eyes, they scream for release from this twisted body he now inhabits.

"I recognize you, now," I say.

He frowns, not expecting that. Some of the demons behind him are agitated.

From the depths of my heart I find these words. "I see the pain in you still, almost as if you were *caught up in forces you can not control. If you are unsure, why not join us as a Neutral Angel."*

One of my fellow angels cringes, and I am embarrassed by that action. It is not lost on the leader either. He looks down at his body. "Be truthful. You would not want one such as me to be a member of your band."

My actions are instinctive. I reach out and hug him. I am not repulsed, I see only a soul in need, my lost friend, another of God's children.

There is a demon beside him. "I feel like I made a mistake, too," he says meekly.

"Shut up!" yells another. "Kill them all now before they poison your minds with Heavenly dribble."

"Wait," I say. I look at the bleak surroundings, the dark caverns around us. Holly and the others are nervous, they do not understand the danger we are in. I decide to try bargaining. "Let the others go," I ask. "Help me complete my mission and I will stay here among you."

"What?" says Holly. "Then, you really are Lucifer's brother."

"Yes," I say to her, turning to face her. "I am his brother. Nothing can change that fact. I also love him, and nothing can change that. I do not share his world and his ideas, but if it will buy you and the rest of the Neutral Angels safety, then it is a bargain I can live with."

"I don't like it," she says.

"Neither do I," says Irin.

We huddle together and I quietly try to make my point.

"It will avoid conflict," I say. I lower my voice to a whisper. "Have you looked around? We are outnumbered, unwilling to fight, and unarmed. What choice do we have?"

"We can stand together," she says.

"It's no so bad," I say, looking around. "My brother should be here soon. At least I will be with family," I add with a grin.

She smiles. "Do you always see the bright side of things?"

"When I can," I say.

The demon leader approaches and we break the huddle. He walks confidently up to me and puts his arm on my shoulder. I flinch, thinking he is going to harm me.

He retracts his hand. "No," he says, calming my fears. "No violence. I thought about what you said. I wanted to know if I could join you. I would consider it an honor to help." His words contain some kind of mysterious power. He says them as if they were an oath of allegiance.

I start to answer him, my mouth beginning to say 'yes' with a smile, but something happens.

I believe all it takes is an admission, an affirmation of what you wish to do with your life, but in this case the words hold more than an empty promise. He feels them in his heart. It begins to glow, and as he rests his arm on my shoulder, it completes a circuit. My heart glows, as does the Grail, and suddenly his form is cast off, melting around him until only his old shape remains. He is a handsome angel, standing tall again, his wings spread as if they had been locked in confinement. "Praise God," he says.

One of the demons screams. "Watch it, they have a magic weapon."

"It can make us slaves of Heaven again," yells another.

There is panic and the cavern comes alive. Thunder erupts in the darkness, footsteps beating the ground as they scurry off. The demons hiss and scream, whooping as they flee, all but a few. The remaining ones slowly come forward, reaching for the Grail.

I do not let them waver; instead I reach out and grab them up in my glowing spirit. The leader joins me, laughing as he throws his arms around us. One by one we find seven new members for our band.

"I am Malchoir," says the leader.

"I remember you now," says one of the Neutral Angels, reaching out to embrace him.

"How did you do that?" Malchoir asks me.

"It is the power of the Grail," I answer. "The power of God's blood.

"It's not just the Grail," says Holly. "It is the power of love and forgiveness. It takes one pure of heart to use the Grail in such a manner."

"So Malchoir is pure at heart?" I ask.

"No, silly," she says. "It is you. I saw your heart begin to glow when you invited him to join us, before you even volunteered to stay with them in exchange for our safe passage. You are the one blessed as pure at heart."

A few demons remain, watching closely from behind rocks. They scatter, fearful that the Grail will transform them into mindless angels. I laugh, thinking that free will guarantees that they will not be mindless. I guess it is a matter of perspective.

Our newest members begin to glow, emitting the faint beginnings of the Light from Within.

"Thank you," says Malchoir. He grabs my arm with a smile. The transformed angels with him nod gratefully.

"Now back to our mission," I say. "I don't want to be here when my brother arrives. He can be frightening at times, and I fear he has found new powers which he may use to harm us."

"Let's go, then," says Holly. "And quickly." We gather up our equipment as we watch the last of the Fallen Ones scurry off towards the darker corners of the cavern.

"I didn't want to ask you about the mission in front of the others, but where are we headed?" asks Malchoir.

"There is a cave at the center of the Sacred Mountain", answers Holly. "We seek it as a resting place and a place of safety for the Grail."

"I know that place," says Malchoir.

"If you know it, what's to stop the Fallen Ones from looting the treasure once we leave it behind?" I ask.

"Don't worry," says Malchoir. "There is something about that cave that makes us uncomfortable. We discovered it as we explored this place. You'll see when you get there. We're close to it now."

I look at Holly and she nods in agreement.

"Where are we exactly?" asks one of the Neutral Angels.

"On the other side of a place we call Hell," answers Malchoir.

"Hell?" I ask.

"It is the name we call our kingdom," says Malchoir. "I'm sorry, it is the name the Fallen Ones call their new home. I am no longer one of them."

I clap him on the shoulders, right between his wings, and we both smile.

44 The Truth Revealed

Malchoir leads the way, Holly and I behind him with the others following. The tunnels are dark and we move between a series of underground chambers. Malchoir has some kind of night vision that allows him to see extremely well in the dark. He is able to peer deep into the distant shadows, taking us directly towards the openings that lead into the next chamber.

Holly stays close to me. She is filled with questions. "Why didn't you tell me Lucifer was your brother?" she asks.

"I told you I have a brother," I said.

"But you didn't tell me he was Lucifer"

"How would you have treated me knowing that fact?" I ask.

"The same way I treat you now, knowing that fact," she replies.

"And how is that?" I ask.

"As a friend," she says, reaching out for my hand. "Is this the burden you would not share?" she asks.

Hiding the truth from her seems pointless. "Yes," I reply flatly.

She is silent for a while. "I see your problem," she says. "Betray your God or betray your brother."

"You speak as if you know me," I say.

"I sense things," she says shyly. "It's part of being an Angel of Mercy."

Malchoir joins our conversation, thankfully making it less personal. "What is the purpose of this Grail object?" he asks, understandably curious.

I tell him the story explaining the origin of the Grail, how the blood of God came to be contained in the simple cup at my hip.

"I see why it's so important," says Malchoir. "But why go to all this trouble?"

"The Grail must be hidden somewhere below the Firmament," says Holly. *"The safety of the Grail is our most important concern. It opens the path back to Heaven, and without it there would be no hope of salvation for anything that exists in this realm."*

"How do you know that?" I ask.

"I've made a few forays in to this realm," she says. *"I've learned a thing or two exploring this place."*

"No, not that," I say. *"You speak of the Grail as if you had known of it all your life. How do you know so much about it?"*

"Why, from the legend, of course," she says.

"What legend?" I ask.

"The legend of the Grail?" she asks, as if I should know all about it. When I don't answer, she continues as if it were scripture. *"A time will come when God must shed His blood for all Creation so as to nourish and protect It from passing into oblivion. And lo, an angel shall carry the blood in a sacred relic to a far off realm, that it may bring salvation to all who seek it. He who fights cannot hold it, he who loves cannot deny it. The power of*

the Grail will be known and sought. Let it be taken to a place of sanctuary lest it be corrupted and forgotten, guarded for all eternity, kept for all time, in service for all Creation."

I am silent.

"Seems like I heard something like that," says Malchoir.

I turn and stare at him for a moment. "Why have I not?"

Holly is both astonished and amused. "Seriously," she says.

Malchoir laughs too. "So, the Grail Angel himself doesn't know of his role in destiny."

They both laugh. "God works in mysterious ways," she says.

As we walk I notice changes in Malchoir. His posture has improved and the light within grows as bright as in any of us. The air around him is radiant and full of energy. His demonic laugh has become a genuine smile.

He notices it too. *"I feel better the further away from Hell that we get."*

"You look better, too," says Holly.

"Thanks."

"We appreciate your help, Malchoir," I say. *"Your ability to see into the darkness is uncanny."*

"A strange thing to retain," he says. *"It was the first ability I noticed after my fall. I actually sought darkness and hid from the light."*

"Strange," says Holly. *"What other changes did you notice?"*

"You mean, besides my body?"

"That change is obvious," says Holly. *"All angels have special abilities. I'm more interested in that."*

"The dark angels can sense each other, just as we sense each other, only stronger," he says. *"We hear voices in our heads, constant chatter that interferes*

with our thinking. Then there is the fire of agony in our hearts."

"Fire of agony?" I ask.

"A pain so great it cannot be imagined. As a heart can feel joy, ours is tuned to malevolence. Our hearts tell us the only way to escape the pain is to cause others to suffer. From that, we feel a fleeting joy, but it is quickly consumed by the fire, leaving only emptiness and burning again."

There is sadness in his eyes as he recalls this. He touches his heart as if he could still feel the fire. The light within dims.

"Does the darkness call to you?" I ask.

"Not anymore," he says. "Tell me, can you see those demons that have been following us?"

"Demons are following us?" says Holly. Alarm spreads through our group.

I peer into the darkness, activate all my senses, but I can see nothing following in our wake. "How far behind?" I ask.

"Just out of our light," he says. "Don't worry, they will come no closer. I sense they are filled with a mixture of fear and curiosity."

"Will the Grail be safe?" I ask.

"It is the Grail they fear, my friend," says Malchoir. "I know the place we are going," says Malchoir. "It is a special place, I will grant you that. The Grail will be safe there."

"But if the fallen know where it is," begins Holly.

"They won't. They will tire and drop back as we approach our destination," says Malchoir.

"You're certain of this?" I ask.

He smiles cryptically and changes the subject. "Tell me more about this place. I have been near it, but never in it."

"It is at the very center of the Sacred Mountain," says Holly.

"What makes this mountain sacred?" he asks.

"The mountain is a bridge where Heaven touches the Earth, rising through the Firmament to link both worlds."

"Is Hell part of the Sacred Mountain?" I ask.

"It seems so for now," says Malchoir. "But the realms beneath the Firmament are still forming. As an Angel of Light, I made many excursions and have noticed that things change here, often suddenly."

"He's right," says Irin. "As a Watcher, I know that to be true."

Holly nods in agreement. "Hell is close to the Sacred Mountain, but not part of it," she says. "We have circumvented the mountain and been beyond the other side. The caves led us on a twisted path to our destination."

"I don't think I could find my way again," I say.

"Don't worry, I can. We should be there soon," says Malchoir. "This way"

He points into the darkness and we trudge along, all weary to the point of exhaustion. We stop to rest and hear noises from the path behind us.

"Fallen Ones," says Malchoir. "I told you they were following."

"Let's keep going," says Holly.

There is no argument. The way is silent for a while, except for our footsteps echoing inside the cave. Occasionally there is wind, strong and fierce. I do not know from where it comes, but it is oddly comforting, as if it were the Breath of God refreshing our spirits.

It is a journey through loneliness and darkness unlike our earlier experiences. No pits of fire, no steam or cold water, and no odor of brimstone. Only the emptiness of a long and tiring walk.

Finally we arrive at a small alcove. At the back of the alcove is a restriction that leads into a chamber that is circular with a high dome ceiling. The room is big enough for maybe twenty or thirty angels to fit inside comfortably.

"I'm not getting sick this time," says Malchoir with a smile.

"What do you mean?" I ask.

"Last time I was here I felt ill," he says. "All of us did."

"You had become a creature of darkness," Holly explains. "This place vibrates with positive energy. I don't know why, but it is a favorable environment for angels and for the Grail itself."

"A bright light hurts an eye accustomed to darkness," I say, "So might this chamber hurt anyone not used to the clear light of Heaven."

In the center of the room is a raised square stone, a natural table or alter upon which to rest my burden. I take the cloth off of the Grail and spread it on the table, then place the sacred relic on the stone. The plate still rests on top of the cup.

"You succeeded," says Holly. "You protected it from danger and brought it to safety."

"WE brought it to safety," I emphasize. I breathe deep and relax. "Quite a journey to get here. I am grateful." I kneel before the alter and humble myself. Others follow suit. The Grail begins to glow, and the chamber is soon filled with a warm light that emanates from it. We stare at it for a while, as one might stare into a warm fire. Some remain on bent knee, others stand with bowed heads and put hand to heart, but all of us give thanks.

"I know it will be safe here," says Malchoir. "But I would like to stay here and guard it. I fear we have not heard the last from my former kinsmen."

"Let us not forget Lucifer," says Irin.

"What about the band of Fallen Angels following us," I say. "Does anyone know where they are now?"

"I'll go back outside into the caves and check," says Gethel.

"I'll go with you," adds Satarel.

"A good idea," says Malchoir. "Perhaps you wouldn't mind a little sentry duty. We manged to lose the Fallen Ones that were following us back in the wind caves. The sounds masked our passage, *but given time and random exploration, there is a chance they may discover us."*

"There will be many who seek the Grail, not all for noble purposes," says Irin.

"How can you be so sure that we lost them in the caves?" asks Holly.

"I sense them," says Malchoir.

"Likewise, can't they sense us?" I ask.

"No," says Malchoir. "When you came out of the waterfall, it was a total surprise." He closes his eyes and breathes deep. His voice becomes misty. "I sense the Dark Ones in the cavern of thunder now. They have posted a guard, only a few, but most have left in fear."

"Fear of the Grail?" asks Holly.

"Yes," says Malchoir. "I pray for my Fallen brethren, having been one of them. I understand their fear. To become like me, changed by the Grail. It puts us in conflict with the fire of the damned that infects our hearts. This fire of agony fills our minds with self doubt and affirmations of unworthiness. At least,

that's what it was like from my experience. I don't know if it's the same for all of us."

"It is noble of you to volunteer, Malchoir," says Holly. "You are the best equipped angel for the job."

"But it may be a long time before anyone comes by to check on you," says Irin. "It will be a lonely job."

"Then I'll stay with you," comes a voice. It is the same angel who had cringed at the thought of Malchoir joining our band when he was as a Dark Angel.

"I am Bat(h) Qol," she says, "Also known as the Heavenly Voice." She is filled with humility as she looks into Malchoir's eyes. "This journey has taught me that we are all brethren still, Fallen or otherwise. Forgive me my prejudice, I have erred and my thoughts were unbecoming of an angel. Will you still have my company?"

Malchoir claps her on the back, right between her six wings. "I am always happy to be in the company of Seraphim," he says.

"Please," she replies. "I no longer think of myself as Seraphim. I am a Neutral Angel, despite my origin."

"As am I," says Malchoir. "Despite my origin." His lips curl gently into a smile, his face relaxes, free of the weight of sin, as light as an angel. "I'm glad you're staying. You must teach me about the Neutral Angels."

"Only if you teach me about the Dark Ones."

"You were never alone, Malchoir," says Shas-ed-dim, one of the converted dark angels who served under Malchoir.

"My trusted Lieutenant," says Malchoir. "We fought together at the prime attack. It was our job to guard the rear and secure Lucifer a path of retreat."

"I witnessed the creation of the Grail," says Shas-ed-dim. He turns to me. "I saw you catch the blood of God. I was wrestling a cherub and we both saw it. We stopped fighting, looked into each other's eyes and shared tears for a moment. Then one of my foot soldiers stabbed him with a short blade. I have not felt well since then and the incident left me lacking in spirit. The Grail has restored all that and more."

More volunteers speak up, testimonials to the power of the Grail.

"I witnessed the Grail creation too," says Kadir Rahman. "I was one of the Dark Ones redeemed by the power of the Grail in the cavern of thundering water." He turns to his former leader. "I was with you then, Malchoir, and I am with you now."

"We talked about it and decided we both want to stay with you," says Shas-ed-dim.

"Together we possess the Power of Faith and Mercy," says Kadir Rahman. "The Grail spoke to me. It is my duty to remain here with you."

Malchoir smiles, his relaxed, angelic smile that radiates as much warmth as the Grail itself. "Of course you can stay. Anyone is welcome."

Two neutral Cherubim step forward, unchanged by Gods commands, these are true Holy Beasts. Again we see Malchoir's smile. "What would a holy relic be without Cherubim guarding it?" He turns to me. "We are seven now, a sacred number, chosen by the Grail. You are free, my friends. Your mission is complete. Fear not, we will guard it well."

"I would pass through Hell again to bring this holy relic to safety," I remark.

"And I would go with you again," says Holly. We have a moment of prayer and thank God for the sacrifice of His blood. "With the Grail in place, Heaven on Earth is now attainable."

"Just as we have attained a moment of Hell in Heaven," adds Malchoir solemnly.

We all think of the bloodshed, saddened at the loss of friends and relatives, families divided along lines. How many others besides Malchoir yearn for a second chance?

"Amen," I hear someone say. We rise and set ourselves straight.

"Thank you for your help," I say to Malchoir. "You made things easy on us."

"And you have set a standard for me," he says. "I see what a pure heart can do. You have infected me, and I am ever grateful for catching that disease."

I draw close to him and we hug. There are tears in his eyes as we pull apart. My enemy has now become my friend, and I can think of nothing more satisfying. There is always hope, even for the Fallen there is a path open to redemption. "Now, how do we get out of here?" I ask, thinking about the long journey home. I shudder at the thought of going through Hell again.

"This is the easy part," says Holly. "Just grab my hand. Everyone who is leaving grab a hand." All but the sacred seven lock hands.

I reach out and touch Holly. The room begins to spin. "What's happening?" I ask.

"Focus on the Grail," she says. "Do you feel yourself getting lighter?"

I do feel something, a strange tingle that begins in the center of my stomach and spreads outward. "Think of the Light, think of our friends waiting for us at the outskirts of the Firmament, think of leaving this cavern," she says. "Concentrate."

We suddenly become transparent, light and free of the pull of the Earth. We begin to float up to the top of the cavern, a stream of angels bound by touch. As we near the ceiling I feel a pang of fear, but Holly turns and smiles, laughing at my fear.

We strike the top of the cave and keep going, passing through the solid rock as if it were water. It is a strange feeling, my vision altered. I see through the rock, up into the light of day that stretches above. We float until we break the surface, emerging into the clear land above. The sun warms us as the wind blows the stale scent of the underworld off our skin.

I float for a moment, my wings spread, my hand locked with Holly's, part of a ribbon of angels. I feel complete in this moment. Our lives have many such moments; call it an epiphany or a peak experience, exhilaration, but it brings us closer to the heights to which our souls aspire. Holly is right. Had I not faced these recent challenges, I would not know this feeling I have now. Without the struggle there is no sense of accomplishment.

I know in this moment what it means to be a Neutral Angel. We are the spiritual path that lies between pairs of opposites, between fear and desire, between good and evil. In short, we are the balance between Heaven and Hell. We are just as much a part of the divine plan as any other creature.

We materialize, if that's what you want to call it, becoming solid again.

"What just happened?" I ask Holly.

"We are angels," she says smiling. "We have always been able to do that."

"Then why did we go through all that torture?" I ask. "Why didn't we just float down there?"

"Obviously, you've never brought something from Heaven below the Firmament," she says. "Whenever angels carry a heavenly object by hand, it remains solid. That's how it becomes a part of the realm to which it's taken. The price of doing this is our transparency and our ability to pass through dense matter, like rock for instance."

"Yes. I see," I say. "I thought the Sacred Mountain had something to do with it too."

"You're right. At times it takes away some of our angel powers, other times it grants us new ones. You'll get used to it the more you come here. It takes time to acclimate. Just like Earth wings require time to develop, so does the ability to move easily outside Heaven," she says.

"But I've been here before," I say.

She makes a cute little noise, a sputter. "In a sacred vessel, I heard you say. That's quite a different thing, I daresay. It would have been nice to travel in an insulated sphere or something. Totally relaxed and free of any maladies or exposure to the harsh environment. Golden stairway to climb down out of it. Next time, maybe you can arrange one for us?"

I don't know if she is being serious or sarcastic. Her wry smile gives me no clue either. I just grin and shake my head.

She is a delightful angel.

"Silly, look at yourself," she says. "You're floating. Just enjoy it."

She is right. I float above the ground, hovering as I would in Heaven, exhilaration born out of being free of the caves. My wings wave gently, unnoticeable and as automatic as breathing. But it is a relative feeling. I look down at the brown, scarred Earth. Volcanoes spew dust and the air above us grows dark, blotting out the sun. Like a great mist of unknowns, the world has quickly turned to a murky reality which easily populates our fears.

Something red and blotchy comes down out of that mist. There is a streak beside us that lands with a *deafening thud. As the smoke clears we hear a horrid scream emerge from the center of a black crater, answered by screeching in the distance.*

"A freshly Fallen Angel," I say.

The creature hisses at us. We hear the screeches in the distance again.

"The call to assembly," says an angel beside me. "Semjaza," he says, introducing himself. "I'm one of the Fallen you saved. I know that one down there. Do you think you can help him?"

"Call to him," I say.

"Focalor," he yells.

The demon looks at us with fiery eyes of hatred. His body tenses, ready to pounce on us and tear us apart with his claws.

"Focalor," says Semjaza, his voice gentle, as if addressing a child. He extends his hand. "Focalor, come with me."

The fire falls out of Focalor's eyes. He is confused.

Semjaza explains, "Yes, I was once Fallen, but there is hope, my friend. We can find grace again."

There is a cry in the distance, a shriek. The demon's pointed ears turn in unison. He roars a response.

"Yes, Focalor. I hear it too," says Semjaza. "But do you not also hear the call of Heaven?"

Focalor shuts his eyes.

I hear it too, we all do: the faint song of Seraphim, the Almighty "Holy, Holy, Holy". It is an important part of the melody that the Universe makes as it moves through its journey in time. When Focalor opens his eyes again, the hatred is gone, the fire replaced with soft, brown eyes that reflect a deep seated soul.

The cry comes again, a bone jarring shriek that bores into the brain. Focalor is shaken. He looks down at his body and there is sadness in his eyes. They gloss over with tears. The cry comes again and the fire returns, evaporating the pain and the tears, turning it to anger. He roars.

"Focalor," says Semjaza. He moves toward the beast but it pivots, roaring one last time at us before it turns and runs with the fury of a raging storm toward the source of the shriek. "Focalor," says Semjaza, his voice lower, filled with sadness. He nods. "Focalor," he says in a slow, quiet breath.

There is another shriek and a thud.

"Another Fallen Angel," I say.

"Come," says Holly. "We better get out of here."

An angel places an arm around Semjaza. "We can't save everyone," she says. "Besides, they must first have the desire to be saved. You have shown your friend that it is possible. The rest is up to him."

45 The Way Home

"I'm lost in all this gloom," I say. "Which direction do we go?"

"Come," she says. "Hold my hand and I'll guide you."

We glide through the air, breaks in the dark clouds below offering glimpses of the world. It is a violent place, still forming, slowly cooling after millennia of pressure in the hands of the Creator. Before long, I see familiar landmarks.

"Let's set down in that meadow," says Holly.

"Good," I say. "My wings are tiring."

I am not alone in this complaint. We set down and rest for a moment.

There is a meteoric whine overhead. Something streaks above like a falling star, but we know what it is. Another thud in the distance, the awful shriek. The volcano rumbles in the distance, fire and smoke cloud our vision.

"I'll go up ahead and scout things out," says Holly. "We're done drifting. We walk from here."

"I'll go with you," I say.

"Stay here and rest," she says.

She's quick, up and down the path before I can protest. But I have rested enough. I rise and run after her. The path twists and enters a narrow canyon, steep rock on both sides. I follow along, feeling I am being watched.

I know where I am. I come to the tight and narrow path between the stones, the trail we started upon so long ago. I glance behind me at that downward path, thinking of the lake of fire and the treacherous caves beyond.

"We're not safe yet," says Holly.

She startles me, sneaking up behind me like that. Serves me right for not focusing my awareness.

There are noises around us. She pulls me forward, a few steps further and we are out of the canyon. I no longer feel the dense rock closing in around me. There is a dark fog; we are unable to see much through the smoke. We move to the right and crouch behind a patch of bushes. Holly sniffs the air, her senses keen and sharp. I can see it in her posture and in the way she carries herself. Her whole body becomes a charged particle stretching out with invisible feelers, sensing the murkiness with a deep awareness. "This way," she whispers, changing direction until she leads us directly to two angels hidden beside some rocks. I recognize Basus and Jekusial, two of the Neutral Angels who stayed behind to guard our retreat.

"Get down," says Jekusial. We settle in beside him.

"Was the mission a success?" asks Basus.

"Completely," says Holly.

"Where are the others?" asks Jekusial. "Everyone safe?"

"They're hiding back there," she says. "The meadow at the other side of the canyon. We came ahead to scout and see if it is safe."

"It is," says Jekusial. "For now."

"What does that mean?" I ask.

"The hills are crawling with Fallen Ones," he says. "They have been falling ever since you left. They come in waves. You just missed another heavy rain of them. The way back to Heaven is clear for the moment, but you'd better hurry."

"Yes," adds Basus. "You stay here with Jekusial and observe. We know this area well. I'll go to the meadow and get the others."

There are nods of agreement. We watch as our friend disappears in the dark fog as he heads towards the pillars. We move quickly and quietly towards the point ahead, the place where we had first descended. This is the base of the trail back up to Heaven. We traverse a small open area. The fog parts for a moment and I notice I am standing on a precipice. I look out and see darkness and destruction.

"Eden is the other way," she says. "Still, this is far from the view we saw coming down."

"Where have the warmth and sunlight gone?" I ask.

"Perhaps the Fallen have brought this violence and unrest to Earth," says Jekusial. "I prefer to have it here than in Heaven." As if in verification, a volcano explodes in the far distance and the ground trembles. Lava flows out of the cone.

"The Earth too spills its blood," says Holly.

Fog drifts around us. It passes like clouds in patches, giving us glimpses of things around us.

"Is this gloom everywhere?" I ask.

"It comes and goes but, yes, it's pretty much everywhere," he says.

"Even in Eden?" I ask.

"Not sure," he answers. "Why? Are you concerned about Man?"

"He is an issue in this fight," I say. "Lucifer has made that much clear."

"We hear that God dispatched Cherubim to guard the sacred garden."

"That will terrify Man more than Lucifer," says Holly.

"Perhaps," I say, studying our situation. Man is suddenly the least of my concerns. Ahead is a steep wall, and next to that the tiny path that etches itself into the side of the mountain. I remember the climb down through the Firmament and dread the trip back up. "That's our only retreat," I say, pointing to the path.

"It's the easiest way back to Heaven," she says. "We'll have to make the slow climb back through the Firmament. Many of us are too weak to fly let alone walk."

"Has anyone come down the path from Heaven?" I ask.

"No," answers Jekusial. "The Dark Ones are falling, cast out of Heaven violently. Haven't seen anyone walking or flying. The only things on Earth now are us and the devils."

Basus arrives with the rest of our band. I signal him and he nods back in understanding. He moves the last of our group out of the narrow canyon, secluding everyone closer to us behind nearby rocks. We are ready to make our move.

There is sound above us as something streaks through the air. A nearby thud and we turn to see a Fallen Angel lying prone on the ground, a crater of dust around him. His body is deformed. He has a pointed tail, horns on his head, and a foul odor about him. He lays still and quiet for a moment, then slowly lifts his head. There are ugly scars and dark stripes across his face, and his chin is elongated and misshapen. Upon seeing us he screams, startled with fear, perhaps because we outnumber him. He jumps to standing and scurries about, looking urgently to embrace any of his fallen comrades.

There is another thud, and this time an even more hideous shape falls before us. This demon is red with yellow teeth and large, jaundiced eyes filled with a misty fright. He shudders, vibrating in a strange, unfamiliar way, almost as if he is a blurred figure painted on a dim canvas. He shudders again, clearly defined yet without shape, quickly blurring in and out of reality.

"This is strange," says Holly.

"We should make a run for the path while we have a chance," says Jekusial. "Leave this nightmare realm behind."

"Shh," I say. "Be quiet and observe."

The foul-smelling demon stops running in circles and stares at the smelly one. There is a shudder. The blurred shape comes back into focus. There is something fresh and meaty dripping from his jaws. He looks at us and then the smelly one. After tense moments of eye contact, Smelly takes off running, dashing for the tight and narrow path between the stones. The newcomer shudders, then comes into focus and runs after him, chasing him like prey, howling as he follows him down the path. Screams and howls echo back at us from the rock crevice, fading to a din in the distance.

We scan the skies, afraid we may be struck by another falling angel. Our group comes out of hiding. The meadow is ours for the moment.

"Time to begin the journey home," says Holly.

"Irin, you know the way," I say. "Why don't you lead? Holly and I will make sure everyone gets away, then we'll follow."

Basus and Jekusial nod. "We'll stay with you for a while."

The angels form groups, tying themselves together with ropes, preparing for a safe ascent. I see many *new friends leave in the first wave: Semjaza, one I saved who then tried to save a fallen comrade. Narshinha, now called the Angel of Heroism after the daring rescue of Gethel from the pit of darkness in the cave. Irin, the Watcher, trusted guide and voice of reason. I learned so much from all of these angels.*

Kzuiel brings Holly and I supplies, ropes and safety gear. "You'll need these," he says. "My group is ready to depart. I'll see you both in Heaven."

There is a shrill sound and a thud, another Fallen Angel. He is covered with black feathers and in place of a nose he has a sharp beak designed for pecking and tearing. His eyes are crossed, looking upon his nose in disbelief. He raises his hands to his face as if to wipe the horror away, but he finds only feathered stumps of wings in which to try.

"What goes?" I ask. "Have you any news of Heaven?"

He lets out a squawk, a horrifying sound that grates our nerves. His mouth moves as if to speak, but only a squawk emerges.

"You no longer have the gift of speech," I say.

Out comes another squawk, this one echos torment, a piteous sound of defeat. He too flees down the path of darkness.

"I gather by his retreat that the Fallen Ones have taken a loss," I say.

"You haven't heard?" says Kzuiel. "Michael won a victory on the Plains of Heaven."

"So that's where all these Fallen are coming from," says Holly. "What about the Creator?"

"No news from the Throne of Heaven itself," he says. "We fear God may still be in danger. There has been no sign of Lucifer, either, not that I would recognize him if I saw him. I'm not being rude, but there have been some pretty ugly sights around here. I can only imagine what twisted form God would visit upon the architect of this war."

"I wonder too," I say, thinking, "My brother! What have you gotten yourself into?"

"Look, the way is clear," says Holly. "You should try to make a run for it."

Kzuiel nods in agreement and gathers up another group. One last team is forming and I encourage Basus and Jekusial to join them. "Thank you for guarding the path," I say to them. "There are some angels unaccounted for. Phanuel, for one. Pedael, Yael."

"I saw Yael in the first group," says Kzuiel.

"Okay," I say. "But there may be other stragglers. I know some stayed behind voluntarily, but it seems our numbers are much smaller than when we started."

"It would seem so," admits Kzuiel.

"That's enough reason for me to remain here for a while and wait for them, just as you waited for us."

"That's a good idea," says Jekusial. "I wouldn't want anyone left behind. Earth is a harsh place, unfit for angels. I'll be happy to leave it."

"Me, too," says Basus. He looks solemnly at me and we embrace. "Thank you for letting us be a part of this. I will see you back in Heaven."

I turn to Holly. "I didn't mean to volunteer you to stay here. I'll be okay on my own. If you hurry up and get ready, you can leave now. The last team is preparing to depart."

"I'm going to stay here and wait with you," says Holly.

"It might be dangerous," I say.

"It will be better if she stays with you," says Kzuiel. "It will take two of you to stand guard. Besides, she knows the way back to Heaven better than any of us. If you go behind those rocks," he points nearby, "You'll be able to see both paths and remain hidden. Oh, and keep an eye peeled upward for more falling angels."

I nod and he is off along with the rest of his band, leaving only Holly and I, alone in the alien environment we now face.

46 The Earth Trembles in Fear

The air is filled with eerie bouts of silence broken by an occasional scream or a tremor. Distant volcanoes announce their presence, spewing dark clouds filled with smoke and cinders. The wind howls at times, deafening the sound of anything approaching. Then, there is the occasional Fallen Angel. But always in between, eerie silence.

The wait is long. We pass few words, instead we stay quiet and observant. We hear strange footsteps, not the tread of an angel, but something heavier. We go deeper into hiding until we hear them no more. We huddle close to each other in the silence that follows.

I look into Holly's eyes and see a sparkle that feeds my soul. In this dreary place it is the only joy. I smile, and she puts her hand to my chest, imparting some of her angelic powers to me. My heart feels light, my burdens eased and my fears erased. All that remains is an ache to know her.

Everything will be fine as long as she is with me. I am so grateful, thankful for her presence. I mutter a prayer to God, feeling more like an angel of protection. She sees my lips moving and dips her face towards mine, joining me in prayer.

I look into her eyes and see myself reflected. When I peer deeper my image moves out of focus and I see her for who she is. I share her dreams, her aspirations as an angel. She smiles and I nod yes. We have been through so much together.

I cannot describe an angel's kiss, it must be experienced. True love on Earth comes close. Holly and I share something that rises from the depths of our souls and crashes upon reality with all the fury of a torrential rain. Afterwards, the connection between us is obvious, the shared thoughts but a pool of stewing ideas. In moments like these time passes in an instant, even as it seems to move slow as it crawls forward with infinite patience.

"Hello," we hear someone call. "Anyone here? Holly?"

"The others have returned," she says, popping her head up to see. I stand and we identify ourselves, beckoning them to hurry.

"Quickly," I say. "The way is clear, but you must come now." They hasten their pace.

"Are there any others?" I ask.

"We are all that are coming," says one of them. "The room has been sealed, and those left behind lie locked within."

"They know what they are doing," says Holly. "Sealing the vault will afford additional protection from the Fallen Ones.

"Yes," I say. "It will remain safe and hidden until it is needed again."

We share our supplies and urge the angels to begin the trek up the path to Heaven.

"We'll be right behind you," I say. They are quick to harness with ropes. Our goodbyes are short and they start immediately on their journey.

Holly and I lay out the remainder of our supplies and take one last look around.

"Frightful place," I say.

"I don't know," she says. "I think it's beautiful. Dynamic, full of life. There's something here not found in Heaven."

"Yes," I say. "Fallen Angels."

47 Rain of Terror

There is a tremendous crack of thunder followed by a tremor. The Earth shakes violently and a deafening rockslide tumbles down the mountain. Further up the path the angels scurry as rocks fall around them. Holly and I move away from the cliff and back to our hiding place behind the rocks. We are only two but we form a circle of protection.

The wind blows again. Howling. Rain begins to fall, pelting us dark red. It splatters on our wings, bathing us in a shower of blood. The sky cracks again.

The wind ceases. There is an eerie moment of silence and then we hear something above the rain, the sound of Falling Angels. It is a peculiar sound I can not feign to imitate. Screams and shouts mixed with sounds not even an animal would make. To call it a rain of terror would be understated, for there are all manner of twisted shapes that fall around us. Blood red and pus green and inkvine black with scars and horns and boils and festering crevices of pain. They quickly turn red in the rain of blood. Yet among them I can find some part of recognition, some detail that triggers my memory. Sometimes I see it in their eyes, other times in a mannerism, but always with the knowledge that I have been together with these souls in worship. Still I scan them all, fearful of the moment when I might find my brother's eyes behind the mask I seek.

There are more tremors, an aftershock, and then another crack. The rocks fall again, some of them landing on Fallen Angels and crushing them underneath. We watch in horror as they crawl from beneath rocks, painfully morphing until they regain their fallen shapes. Some are not so lucky. A group of devils overturn a boulder that traps one of them. As the trapped soul slithers free he is set upon by his own kind, eaten and consumed as though by wolves. Parts of him merge with the diners, growing out of their sides and heads as part of them. We witness this unholy feast several times, the meadow now full of demons with two heads and six limbs and all manner of type in between. They feast and bathe in the rain of blood, celebrating their fallen state with undue lust. They scream and shout and dance, chanting "Lucifer", their hooves and talons pounding on the grass and turning it to brown, charred pulp. Finally they run off, yelling and howling, heeding the call to assembly that echoes from the canyon between the columns of stone.

Holly and I are alone again. We press close to the lee side of a rock, trying to lessen the sting of the blood rain. There are strange sounds, an occasional crack of lightning, rumbles from the Earth, but soon the angels stop falling and the rocks stop sliding. Now there is only silence. I can hear my own breathing.

I wait a while, poke my head out and scan. "Let's go, Holly," I say, urging her forward.

"I'm right behind you," she answers. We gather up our meager supplies and dash across the meadow.

Then I see him, off to the side watching me. With him it was always the eyes. I see the same intent gaze he always has, betraying a mind that will never stop thinking. Outwardly there is chaos visited upon his body. His feet are hooves, cloven and twisted back at an odd angle. From there, thick bullocks of dark fur cover him to the waist. He has skin above that, blotchy but mostly red as if his skin had been turned inside out. His torso is naked, never again to bear the golden vest of jewels that God had given him. At his back are large dragon wings, thick and leathery, foreboding with their scalloped edges as he extends them and smiles toward me.

In his left hand he holds a spear, a souvenir retrieved by one of his loyal followers after the final battle for control over Heaven. His hand fondles the *shaft and he twirls the head, spinning it between his fingers.*

"We meet, my brother," he says, always the one to initiate a conversation. His voice is different, raspy, like a dry wind against a parched land. I stare into his face. It too is blood red, his ears and chin pointed, twisted horns projecting above his brow. His nose thrusts out like a hawk, but it is his eyes that hold me captive. Like a serpent he traps my gaze. I am hypnotized, nay compelled, into inaction, powerless to do anything but move closer to him. I resist, forcing myself to look away, but I am inevitably drawn to him.

With him is a small band of disciples, snaking behind him into the tight and narrow path that leads between the stones and down towards Hell. I move closer, now under my own volition since it is what he desires. I nod to him while I motion for Holly to leave. She is hesitant, fearful for my safety but I reassure her with a look that I will be all right. Still she does not retreat. I step forward, moving cautiously towards Lucifer as I put myself between them.

I smile and reach out to hug him, but he blocks me with his arm.

"Careful, you'll get the smell of brimstone on you," he says. His breath is thick and heavy as he speaks. "Mustn't soil your beautiful robes."

I look down at my tattered robes, far from beautiful after our ordeal in the caverns. "I don't care," I say, pushing his hand aside. I begin to pull him tight but he blocks my approach again, this time with the staff of his spear.

He scans me from head to toe, affirms my appearance with a disdainful nod. "Then, please don't soil my robes."

I sense something deep from him, a feral scent of fresh, open wounds. Behind the façade of calm lies a restless sea of emotion. He has taken with him all discord from Heaven, and now it lay upon his shoulder like a burden of truth. What can I hope to gain for him?

"Different, we two are," he says.

"Yes," I say.

"Did you ever really agree with me, or were you just toying with me?" he asks.

"I tried to be a mirror for you," I say. "But I am not immune to your influence. I question myself because of you. I still battle myself over things we discussed, so don't say I have been toying with you. If anything, you are toying with me."

He smiles, a grin so wide, so filled with satisfaction and cunning that I am forced to smile as well.

"You say you battle yourself?" he begins, all guile and honey, the rasp fading from his voice. "What was that like? Did you stick yourself with sword or launch an arrow into your calf? Can you show me your scars?"

I don't know what to say. What does he expect of me? I look away, breaking eye contact with him.

"I will miss our conversations," he says. "Are you sure you won't join me? I can offer you a position of power and authority in my kingdom. There will be worlds to dominate, souls to command, a chance for a destiny of your own making. It's more than you would get from..." he shrugs his head towards Heaven, his eyes cast downward at the same time, as if it were blasphemy to look back upon Heaven or even mention the name of God in his presence.

He does not realize that I already have a destiny of my own, that my life is unfolding as it should. "Though your offer sounds tempting, you know I can't accept it," I say. "You know me well enough. We have talked about this at length. In truth I swore an oath of neutrality. I will not raise a sword against you."

He recognizes that fact, and it seems to cleanse the way between us for the moment. His eyes are soft, his smile genuine as he nods. As always, we have gone as far as we can with this line of conversation and he seems to recognize that.

"So, what lies ahead for you?" I ask.

"I have my kingdom." He nods towards the path between the stones.

"I have seen it," I say. "It's quite…. Interesting."

"Yes, I love the venue," he says. "Lakes of fire, pits of darkness, eternal labyrinths, it's everything I've wanted and more. So much to explore, so much I haven't seen. And it's bigger than Heaven, much bigger," he boasts.

"Then, I am happy for you."

There is an awkward silence. I am tempted to say more but I restrain myself. I am painfully aware of what I have learned about the Middle Way. My actions are a two edged sword with consequences that can lead to misinterpretation. Not to mention my brother's penchant for twisting words. As a Neutral Angel I must stay uninvolved in my brother's business. "I will be off then," I say.

"Yes, yes," he says nonchalantly. "You and your companion." He cranes his head. "I like her," he says, staring at Holly over my shoulder. "Though she will never replace me."

"We have more in common than you think," I say. "Would you like me to introduce you?"

"Maybe some other time," he says. "I am in a bit of a hurry myself."

"Oh?" I say, feeling somewhat jilted. But I often misinterpret his abruptness.

"Yes," he says. "I thought I would head down to that garden over there." He points south towards Eden, smiling. "I want to introduce myself to Man, maybe see this new companion that everyone is talking

about. Do you know I have the power to change my shape now?"

"No," I say. "I didn't know that."

"I have many new powers here," he says. "Powers I have yet to discover. I seem to feed upon this realm, drawing strength from its very shape and form. Who knows what I am capable of? But back to Man, the focus of God's attention and thus the focus of mine. I am thinking of disguising myself, perhaps as a serpent. For some reason that shape appeals to me. What do you think?"

When I have no comment to offer, he continues. "I've been pondering something," he says. "What do you think will happen when Man partakes of the fruit of the Tree of Knowledge?"

"Look what it's done for you," I say.

"Yes," he says proudly. "I am Man's great hope. Once I convince him to try the fruit, he will see God for what He is. Oh, don't look so worried. I won't abandon Man like God abandoned the Angels. He'll have a place in my Kingdom. Not as exalted as the angels, but still a place."

"Whatever appeals to you, brother." I remind myself of my neutrality, even when it comes to Man. He sees the spark in my eye, aware of what I am thinking. He always had that gift, too, a kind of second sense about what others are thinking. He leans in close to me, right in my face. I can see the madness in his eye. His pupils are deep, disturbing pools surrounded by yellow, jaundiced sockets. His breath is putrid in his naked state, for he does nothing to hide his true self from me now. His skin is abnormally warm, leaching sweat that sticks to his reddened hide, covering him with glistening beads.

"As you say. Whatever appeals to me." His voice is raspy now, no longer soothing and brotherly, almost as if another personality had suddenly eclipsed his normal state. "One more thing, brother," he says, the words come forth as if made by grating metal on stone. "Don't deceive yourself too long with this dream of neutrality. I am glad that you did not side with God, but in the end you are either with me," he pauses for effect, "or against me." He leans a little closer, nodding his head affirmatively while staring into me.

I will not present him anything but a perfect mirror. I think of unending love, I think of prayer, and again he must see this in me. He backs away, still nodding, standing triumphantly on his hooves, his cape flourishing in the breeze. "You sicken me," he says. "You speak in one moment of neutrality and yet you long to run back to Heaven. Why not remain neutral in my presence? I can still offer you a piece of my kingdom for your own. If that is that what you wish?"

He tempts me with his words, and I wonder if what he suggests is possible. A kingdom for neutrals based on the principles of the Middle Way. Why have I not considered the possibility of living in his world? Then again, in a sense, we have already established a base in this realm: the resting home of the Holy Grail.

"I…" I start to speak but he cuts me off.

"Don't say it. Save it for her," he says, poking his jaw in Holly's direction. "Or better yet," he shouts towards the Heavens, "Save it for Him," he screams. He begins to laugh, gently at first, then becoming more maniacal and menacing. His men look pensive and excited, like a pack of dogs that will turn on anyone who crosses their master. I slowly walk away from him, indicating to Holly that we should leave.

Then he makes a move. While I am not looking he reaches out and snatches my arm, reeling me around to face him once again. "Don't turn your back on me," he says angrily. "I'm not done with *you yet." His skin burns my arm where he tightens his grasp, but I do not flinch. The heat begins to build. He knows he is hurting me, but I will not wince and give him the satisfaction. His smile widens and he focuses his eyes on me intently. "I have a gift for you. Something to remember me by," he rasps. "You speak of neutrality, but I saw everything that transpired. Don't think your little mission is hidden from me. I know everything. You caught the blood of God and even subverted some of my generals. How do you call this neutrality?"*

"I did not raise a sword against you," I say.

"Yes, you didn't," he says, overly facetious. "Fighting is not your way, is it?"

"No," I say. "As for your generals and your men, they made choices of their own free will."

"You never faced The Sword of Fire, did you?" he asks.

"No," I answer again, wondering where he is going with this conversation.

"Let me show you what it is like," he says, pulling me close into his gaze. Within his eyes there grows

a cloud of red, a storm of destruction swelling from the depths of his evil. I do not think he will hurt me, but he is angry and his wrath is out of control. I stare into the hurricanes churning in his eyes, transfixed and hypnotized as if he were a cobra.

The cloud expands and the storm breaks loose, assaulting my mind in a cyclone of terror. I am caught within it, unable to look away, unable to do anything but stare helplessly into the onslaught. From within those eyes pour all the evils he can muster. It is a moment when the dark artist creates his most terrible work, imparting to me every lurid detail of the battle. I experience every stab of the sword, every thrust of a spear, every burning pot of fire. I feel my limbs severed, my skin burn, and my eyes go blind. I stare into the empty faces of the soldiers beside me. I feel Michael's Sword of Fire melt my flesh into demonic shapes. I fall helpless to the ground, blood seeping from gaping wounds that wet my robes.

And then I experience it all over again, this time as the aggressor, a sword or a lance in my hand as I thrust it mercilessly into my foes. I feel myself fighting with claws and talons as I gouge eyes and split entrails. Teeth break and limbs crack with blows from my heavy mace. And then, the most evil of all sensations, I myself thrust a spear that pierces the side of My Creator. The blood is on my hands, the weight of the lance in my arms.

I scream and then withdraw, running like a madman to escape his company. I trip over some stones and fall helpless like a blind child staring into empty space. The vision will not fade. I scream in agony.

"What did you do to him?" yells Holly, running to my side.

He laughs now, an evil wicked laugh that shatters his control over me. But the memories remain, the essence of the battle has retreated somewhere inside me for the moment. I feel it moving like a snake through my insides, feeding on my sanity like some kind of grubworm.

"How do you like my gift, brother," he says. "You did not even have to be there. I have given it all to you, every last perspective, and now you can relive the battle and see exactly what you missed."

I am shivering. "Why did you do this?" yells Holly. "He never harmed you."

"He is my masterpiece," he says. "The living Grail of my blood."

"Why?" shouts Holly. I sense her anger. She is mad enough to fight, mad enough to sacrifice her neutrality. I am ashamed to be the catalyst that triggers her emotions. Is that why he did this thing?

I am shivering. Holly puts her arm around me, helps me up off the ground, and leads me away. We reach the wall without incident. She tethers us together with rope and we start our climb, picking our way carefully upward. We hear him bellow, his words garbled and echoed. I do not know if he is screaming at God or at me, it sounds like so much rage.

It is a long time, an eternity stretches into that climb. I ache and tire, my angelic feet sore from so much walking. We have been smothered in darkness, baked in steam, and cooked in fresh water and now I climb a tight path and I am exhausted from it all.

I hear my brother blaring again, his voice distant but legible. He shouts to catch God's ear. Despite my exhaustion I redouble my effort.

"Why can't we fly?" I ask. Then I have my answer. I shiver, and feel the stab wounds, the fire, and the pain. My stomach leaks from out of my belly and I am back on the Plains of Heaven experiencing the war again. I grip the wall, the path narrow here, a shiver away from plummeting over the side. Holly *holds me tight and close. It passes quickly as she does this. Still weak, I gather myself from my petit mal and nod my assurances to Holly and we set out again.*

As we continue to climb upward and towards Heaven, the Light of Goodness increases, gradually warming my soul. Soon I hear him no more. I feel light, beginning to climb rapidly, yearning for the safety of Heaven.

Holly cautions me, tempering my eager spirit. She is correct. The rock wall is harsh, unforgiving, and I nod to her wisdom.

We continue, slow and careful, but soon we reach the end of our climb. She smiles. Ahead on the precipice at the Gates of Heaven our friends wait for us. They wave, Basus and Jekusial, Irin the Watcher, and Kzuial.

Holly turns, her look triumphant, the glow of Heaven behind her. She reaches out for my hand and I take it as she pulls me up the final step.

Her hand is hot, scaly. The glow of Heaven is now a fire. My friends have changed into hideous demons.

I hear, "Look out, Father."

I look down at the red claw that grasps my hand. It squeezes tight, pulls me closer. "Let me help you there, brother."

48 My Affliction Ordained

My daughter is at my side. "Let go of him," she shouts. "Can't you see you're hurting him?"

"Like he hurt me?" shouts Lucifer. He squeezes my hand tighter, his grip a crushing force.

"No," she says. She speaks to him in a calm voice. "It's different the way he hurt you." He squeezes tighter, then releases, pushing me back. He inspects his hand, brushes it gently, as if cleaning dirt from it.

I nurse my crushed hand. There are calluses and burns.

"Why do you keep hurting him?" she asks.

Lucifer does not respond.

"Aren't you here to answer my questions?" she asks.

He seems to be in a daze.

"I know you're upset," she says. "But why take it out on my father?"

"He was my brother," he says.

"Is your brother," she corrects.

He is angry with her. No one corrects him. He stares back at her, his face contorted, but she is angry, too.

He looks at me. "You never told her," he says.

"Told her what?" I ask.

"About our early adventures. Our missions for God, the places we surveyed and built for the Architect, the improvements we made together to all aspects of life in Heaven."

She is surprised, looking at us both with newfound respect. "If you remember, Uncle, then perhaps you also remember the love you share with my Father? I would like to see those memories."

He sneers. "She is so like you," he says.

"Thank you," she says. "Can you do something for me? Please?"

He is suddenly amused and enamored with her. "Depends on what it is," he says.

"Take my father's pain away. Take the memories of the war away from him."

He is angry again. "I will not. The gift I have given can never be taken back."

"It is not a gift," she says.

"You have no idea, child," he says. He moves close to her and I fear for her safety. "What I gave your father is part of my self. I feel the same things, the same pain, the same suffering every day, every minute of my life. It is the gift our loving Father shared with me, a gift I now share with my brother.

His eyes begin to glow red, storm clouds forming over his pupils. "Would you like a taste of the family pain?" he asks.

"No!" I shout. I put myself between them. "What are you doing? She is a child."

The storm abates.

"Very well," he says. "Tell you what I will do," he says to her. "I will remove the ransom on your father. He is no longer marked and hunted by my clan." He touches the back of my neck and I feel a burning sensation on my forehead. My skin is not marred but it is painful.

He gently puts his arm out and sweeps me aside. She is not afraid of him and they face each other again. "So, you'd like to see some memories of your Father and I?"

"Yes," she says, adding. "But not right now. I've had enough memories. I want to go home."

"Fair enough," he says. "Then, when you're ready, come down to my place for a visit. Take a vacation from your Dad and spend some time with your Uncle Lucifer. We'll share some memories, and make a few of our own."

And he is gone.

49 Home Again

We are in our garden, free of the spell of memories. I rest, tired and exhausted after all we've been through. For me, the story was replayed just as the original. I was trapped in the drama of my own past, experiencing everything as it was. And now my brother's gift again lies on the doorstep of my consciousness begging to be opened.

We are both deep in thought. She finally breaks the silence.

"I think God was angry with Lucifer for falling from His Grace," she says.

"When Lucifer tempted Man and Man fell as well, God became even angrier. He cursed Man with labors, visited plagues upon Him, He even destroyed all but a handful of them in a massive flood. But Man deserved such things, and like an unruly child he invented his own evils, such as the murder of Abel by his brother Cain."

"Uncle Lucifer predicted Man would disappoint God," she says.

"Yes, but don't discount your Uncle's part in that. True, God was angry with Man for some time, but then He passed beyond His anger, returning to His core belief in love and free will. He even wanted to know what it was like to be a man, so He sent His Son to be born and to live among them. Satan tried to tempt His Son, but through His example and His sacrifice He showed Man how to resist darkness and to embrace love. He gave Man hope."

I think about the crucifixion of Christ and recount my role in history. "I was called to duty at His death on a small hill called Calvary. There, events long forgotten above the Firmament were mirrored below. A spear pierced the side of Christ as He hung close to death, and sacred blood was once again spilled and caught in a chalice. The Grails were thus linked, one on Earth and One inside the Sacred Mountain. Power resonates between them, making a bridge from the highest realms of Heaven to the fertile fields of men's hearts, for only the pure at heart can possess the Grail."

She nods in understanding.

"I am pleased. You've grown a lot," I say.

"I've been through a lot," she says.

"There is one more thing you must see," I say. "Are you rested enough for another trip to Earth?"

Her smile says it all. I take her hand in mine and we are off to the gates, plummeting into the Firmament like skydivers.

50 Earth Revisited

It's not long before we emerge into the night skies above the Earth. Below we catch a glimpse of a flashing light as we descend towards it, a speeding ambulance. Behind it several angels fly in quick pursuit. We land on the roof and poke our heads through the top, observing the activity inside. A radio is blaring instructions while a medic hovers over an injured man strapped to a gurney.

"His color," remarks my daughter. "He's so pale."

"His spirit is fading, but he clings to life", I explain. "The flame refuses to die out."

"Why? If he just dies, the struggle will be over," she says. "And he can begin life in Heaven."

The simple logic of the child, I cannot discount it. "If people knew of Heaven and its reward, they would have no will to live, and so they are cast with an instinct for self preservation that fosters a fear of death."

The medics work on the injured man. Next to him is a guardian angel, hand resting gently on his shoulder. The light of his soul flickers around the man, and I hear my daughter gasp. His spirit fades for a second, and then his body glows a bright yellow until it balloons outward, covering him in a bright shell.

Like a crab molting, his spirit rolls free in an aura that rises above the silent body. The soul's eyes widen, as a newborn baby's would. He sees the guardian angel next to him. "I know you," he says.

Machines beep and the technicians work fervently on the body, one administering CPR while the other injects lifesaving drugs into the empty shell. The soul feels a tug, like someone clinging to an old sentimental garment. He tugs back and the fabric snaps. The final decision has been made. The soul and the guardian angel look down at the mortal shell laying on the gurney. They join hands and together they begin their journey to Heaven.

I gently yank at my daughter's side and pull her through the roof of the ambulance where we sit and talk.

"He had a good life," I say.

"How can you tell?" she asks.

"His guardian angel was waiting for him at death, ready to guide him home," I say. "But you can also tell by the color of his soul. His was bright amber, with tinges of violet and blue. His heart was rich with the experience of a full life. And he died without fear, a smile on his face."

"So, not everybody dies in violence," she says.

I smile. "Good. You have already begun to learn what I brought you here to see. What happened on your last visit to Earth was extraordinary."

The siren whelps and startles us. The ambulance accelerates and weaves through the traffic. "Why are we moving faster?" she asks.

"Time is critical," I explain. "They are trying to reach the hospital where they hope to revive him."

"Hospital?" she asks.

The ambulance rounds a turn and stops at an emergency room entrance. A medical team is waiting. They unload the body and race through the doors of the hospital. We follow them inside.

"This is where Man concentrates all his efforts to stave off death," I say. We wander through the emergency treatment rooms, watching doctors and nurses and specialists helping injured people. In some cases angels huddle beside them, some of them skilled at repairing the damaged psychic and spiritual parts of the patients.

We look into the waiting room where anxious family members thumb through magazines, pace nervously, and make sparse conversation. We find a small chapel where a group of people sit silently and pray. In one hallway there are patients in wheelchairs or on gurneys parked behind drawn curtains. The Angel of Death wanders by as he makes an accounting of the endless stream of souls who pass from this life.

We wander into one small room where we encounter a young boy who wears a fresh cast over a broken bone. His tears are finally gone, and he is left with the realization that he will be carrying this stiff, heavy plaster arm for some time. A doctor consoles him while his mother looks on from a nearby chair. He scribbles some notes onto a piece of paper attached to a clipboard, then looks up at the boy and smiles.

"I have to go now," he says. "I have other patients to see, but you'll be okay now." He turns and looks right at my daughter and I as if he could see us. "See, the angels are watching over you," he says.

The boy looks up and smiles, and I raise my arms in prayer. My daughter goes to his side and tenderly touches his cheek. I place a band of healing and protection over him and his mother and then the entire room. The doctor turns and leaves and, now curious, we follow him out into the corridor.

He wipes the sleep from his eyes, thinks about getting a cup of coffee, and instead turns into the next room down the corridor. Inside a nurse is standing over a burned man who twists in pain on a table. She checks his vital signs and inputs them on a computer.

The man's skin is red and dark, much like one of the Fallen. His soul is dark as well. He twists in agony even though he is heavily medicated. He tries to say something but it is unintelligible.

"Look there," I say, indicating him to my daughter. "There is one who has not made his peace with God or himself. See the difference in his color, all black and grey and lifeless."

"Not like the man in the ambulance," she says.

"No, not like him." I bend over the man and pray, placing my hands on his temples. He feels only temporary relief, I'm afraid. With his body burned so badly he struggles to stay conscious.

"I understand his agony. He has betrayed himself. You must know that you cannot lie to yourself. One of the challenges that face humans, and angels I believe, is to discover and overcome your self. The self is like a hurdle that blocks access to God. Living with God in your heart creates balance and helps to better define the self's choices."

The furrows are back again, my role as her father restored. "The battle continues," she says.

"What do you mean?"

"Humans must take an active role," she says. "When Uncle Lucifer and his horde were cast out, it created the schism. Perhaps humans will knit the Universe back together for God.

"I choose to think that there are no sides, that this conflict is merely tension. To walk, to move forward, humans must balance the movements between the right and left sides of their body. So it is on the path, with moral choices on the left and right to balance."

The doctor speaks. "Is this the man who set the fire?" he asks.

"Yes," answers the nurse, looking up at him. "Did the old woman die?" she asks. "The one who came in with the little boy who was burned?"

"Yes. About ten minutes ago," he says sadly. He looks down at the burned man. "How is he doing?"

"Not good. With seventy percent of his body burned I'm surprised he's alive," she replies. "I've administered pain killers and put him on the antibiotic drip. Do you want to order anything else?"

I look into the man's eyes and see the demons that haunt his past. He is a victim of the very fire he set. He watched the child burn before his eyes, his own son. He thought the family was gone. He burned the house for the insurance money, then discovered his mistake. He din't know the boy was upstairs. I say another prayer as I look into his pain. The doctor again acts as if he senses our presence, mysteriously joining us in prayer.

"Why pray for this one, doctor? He's going to Hell anyway," says the nurse.

"Maybe not," replies the doctor. "As long as there is a breath of life left in him, he has a chance. A man can always repent his deeds while he is still alive."

"He's right," I tell my daughter. "Just as you cannot change your past, so you cannot change your life after death. It is written into the record for all eternity. With the gift of free will comes the responsibility to make good choices."

"There is so much suffering here," she says.

"I believe that the battle in Heaven long ago created waves of discord that even now are felt on Earth. It explains why there are so many disharmonies among men. If Heaven can find no rest, is there any hope for Earth?"

"You told me there is always hope, Father."

"There is," I say. "You do not have to be religious to have God in your heart. Going to church nurtures and hastens the process, but so do deeds of mercy and forgiveness. Hope, along with faith and charity, is one of the three divine virtues."

"I know that," she says, smiling.

We leave the room with hope in the air. I grow weary of the scent of death. It hangs in the emergency room air like incense at church. It is time to move on and show my daughter what hope looks like.

We go upstairs, past doctors in operating theaters playing God, past nurses' stations bustling with activity, past streams of visitors carrying wishes to their loved ones. Finally we arrive at a simple operating room, beige tiled floor, green ceiling and walls. To one side lay a woman on a table, her legs up in stirrups while a nervous doctor observes and waits. At her ear, her husband coaches her to breathe as he strokes her forehead in light effleurage. She puffs, short breaths, and then she pushes. My daughter watches in fascination. They don't call it the miracle of life for nothing.

There is nervous tension in the room.

"Is the baby coming now?" she asks.

Off to the side a neo-natal team of specialists wonder if they will be needed. My daughter notices them. "Why are all these people here?" she asks.

"Does it take this many people for a human to be born?"

"This baby is premature," I explain. "He is so anxious to be born that he is coming weeks ahead of his time. There may be complications, and so these people are here to attend to the baby should he need it."

The doctor looks up, into the mother's eye. He nods affirmatively. It is time again.

Her husband whispers gently in her ear. "Here we go. Push."

Even my daughter is tense, her eyes and ears wide with expectation. Some members of the neonatal team shift their weight to the balls of their feet, rocking nervously.

Suddenly the room is filled with crying. A tiny mouth calls out for attention, as if saying for the first time in a primitive tongue, "I am here. I am human." It is a cry of affirmation.

The doctor cuts the umbilical cord, ties it and hands the baby to a nurse. She washes the newborn and wraps it in a clean blanket. The neonatal team inspects the child and disbands, no longer needed. The doctor inspects the baby.

"He's okay," says the doctor, finally handing the baby to the mother. "This baby had an eighty six percent chance of living, most likely six months on a respirator before dying. I'd say he beat the odds."

"It's a miracle," whispers the nurse.

The mother and father smile at each other, then look at the baby, then back at each other. The baby's eyes are bright and eager, true innocence. They say that progeny recapitulates phylogeny, meaning that the evolution of a single soul follows the path of the entire species. Looking into that baby's eyes, I see nothing but the pure Light of Heaven. I wonder how long before that Light will begin to dim, before he mirrors the fall of Man and finds the truth behind the fruit of the Tree of Knowledge of Good and Evil.

My daughter draws close to me. She is deeply moved by this miracle, and she reaches out her arms and touches the baby. He looks up into her eyes, and the parents notice the baby's attention move towards the bright spot that is my daughter. He coos and points with pudgy, wrinkled fingers in her direction.

The parents laugh again, and I can see the fullness of their hearts. This baby makes their life complete. As new parents, they enter a new stage of love, and I am filled with hope. I hope they learn as much as I have learned from love. I hope they enjoy life.

I look down at my daughter feeling a father's pride.

The world, and Heaven for that matter, is filled with opposites. Polarized choices at every turn. Perhaps that is why I prefer the Middle Way, for it is only in the middle that we find balance.

God bless you. May you also find peace and balance on your journey as you walk the narrow path back towards Heaven.

THE END

Satan's Repose

So God, my friend
This is where you banish me
(to Earth)

But You are still my friend
And I love You enough to accept my banishment
For Your guilt
For Your love
of Self

For if I am not a part of You
What am I?
And what is Your Universe
If it is not all inclusive?

Other titles by Nick Delmedico:

Aliens vs. Dinosaurs at the Beginning of Time

Co-authored with Nick Delmedico, his son

The world of dinosaur – 65 million years ago when giant beasts fought each other for dominance of the herd. One monarch has a vision of a better world in which dinosaurs cooperate and live in peace. But that peace is shattered when hostile aliens from another world challenge the dinosaurs for dominion of the Earth. They collect the small ones, the children, taking them away to a distant laboratory where they can be studied.

King Rex finds his daughter is among the missing. As his world crumbles around him, as his enemies circle around him loking for weakness, he struggles to find a way to harness the power of flying without wings. His goal: to send an envoy of peace to the aliens and negotiate the release of the children. Failing that, to take the children back by force using an army of dinosaurs that have united behind him with one cry: Rescue the children.

And, exclusively on Kindle:

Corporate Mercenaries

Could You Please Hold My Baby?

Once Again, Prometheus

www.ingramcontent.com/pod-product-compliance
Lightning Source LLC
Chambersburg PA
CBHW071209250626

47159CB00001B/254